Tales of
Love and Disability

LAURA SOLOMON

Woven Words Publishers OPC Pvt. Ltd.

Registered Office:

Vill: Raipur, P.O: Raipur Paschimbar,

Dist: Purba Midnapore, Pin: 721401,

West Bengal, India.

Branch Office(Operations): Hyderabad

www.wovenwordspublishers.com

Email: publish@wovenwordspublishers.com

First published by Woven Words Publishers OPC Pvt. Ltd., 2018

Copyright© Laura Solomon, 2018

NOVEL

IMPRINT: WOVEN WORDS FICTION

ISBN 13: 978-93-86897-50-3
ISBN 10: 93-86897-50-4

Price: $ 6/ 200 INR

Printed and bound in India by Woven Words Publishers.

Some of these stories and poems have been previously published.

Prosthesis, Aurora Wolf, United States, 2017

Vision, Sentinel, United Kingdom, 2016, Atunis, 2017

Those Left Behind, Blackmail Press, New Zealand, 2017. Jellyfish Review, United States, 2017.

Blood and Guts, The Newsletter of the Association of Literary Scholars, Critics, and Writers, United States, 2015.

Old Hat, Jellyfish Review, United States, 2017

Marsha's Deal, Langlit, India, Landfall, NZ 2017

Boris v Shelob, Landfall, NZ, 2017

The Glass Screen, Sentinel, UK, 2012

The Accidental Time Traveler, Aphelion, United States, 2017

The Orphanage, Adelaide Literary Magazine, New York, Taj Mahal Review, India, 2017

The Scarecrow, LE Poetry, Bali, 2017

The Cellar, Adelaide Literary Magazine, New York, 2017

Cryonics, The Fiction Pool, UK, 2017

Solitary, Punch Magazine, India, 2017

Hitch, Bosphorus Review, Turkey, 2017

The Roofer, Bosphorus Review, Turkey, 2018

The Roofer, Bangalore Review, India, 2018

Special thanks to Brian Shirra, Kerryn Young and Jacquie Mills
for their help with these stories.

Table of Contents

Prosthesis

The new right arm was a welcome addition. He'd lost his old paw by neglecting his diabetes and contracting gangrene from below the shoulder. They'd been forced to amputate or the gangrene would have spread. The arm was black and fashioned from carbon fibre. He was a pianist; it was important that the fingers worked and that the sensors in the fingertips offered feedback. He had complete control over all five fingers. There were tactile pads which controlled how fast the fingers opened and closed. The fake arm used electrodes stuck onto the outside of his upper arm to sense muscular impulses in the residual limb. The signals from these electrodes were picked up by artificial sensors in the prosthetic arm, where a touch and pressure feedback system sent signals back to the brain. He could feel what he was doing without having to look. Artificial nerves; artificial feelings. He could use the hand in the dark.

The socket was carefully mounded around a plaster cast taken from a residual limb. The stump changed shape and size over the years, so new sockets were needed from time to time. The artificial arm was controlled by the brain. When he thought "I want to move my fingers", his brain stimulated muscles in his residual limb to move and the prosthetic arm would shift accordingly. Transhumanism. The hand was strong enough to crush a can. It could be cleaned with baby wipes but was not to be used in a shower or pool. It cost approximately $50,000. He had inherited the money to pay for it from his grandfather who had owned a supermarket chain.

He played on cruise ships. He was a hit with the women. The hand gave them something to talk about. There were ladies, many ladies, cruising the world on their husband's pensions. Predictably, the husbands got jealous. He got tired of playing the same old standards and would occasionally break out into improvised jazz.

It was in 2019, when he had been playing on the ships for two years that it started. At first he thought that he was imagining things, but then it became obvious that he was no longer the leader, he was now the follower. The hand was leading the way, playing on its own, capering around the piano like an out of control pony who had lost its reins. Try as he might to exert his will over it, he could not harness it. The hand had gone wild, broken free.

Something in its programming, no doubt, he thought to himself.

Out loud, to others, he was unsure of what to say. The hand was putting his job in danger. Half of the time the sound it came out with was harsh and discordant - far from easy on the ears. People were vacating the dining hall when he played, getting up and leaving, their meals half finished upon the table. Untamed, set free, the hand was dangerous, like a wild hawk that turns upon its owner.

They hadn't warned him about this in the brochures! This hand could be the death of him if he wasn't careful. It was out of control. It could get him in trouble; get him into very hot water. Unsure of how to handle the situation, he decided to telephone the company responsible for the hand's manufacture.

The phone was picked up after three rings and answered by an efficient sounding voice.

"Good morning Watson and Sons. How can I help?"

"Hello I bought a prosthetic limb from you some months ago and it appears to be faulty."

There was a pause.

"Can you please provide more information Sir?"

"I am a pianist and I rely on my hand to obey instructions from my brain. However, of late, it appears to have developed a mind and a will of its own. It's gone crazy. It's serious. My job is in danger."

"That's no good. Can you provide me with the make and model number please? It's located on the base of the unit."

He took off his limb and looked at the base. The numbers were worn but visible.

"The make is Pros365. The model is Proton3000."

"Thank you very much for that information. What's your phone number please?"

He recited the number.

"I'll look into it and call you back."

She hung up rather abruptly and he was left with the dial tone ringing in his ear.

Time passed and the hand did not modify its behavior. If anything, it got worse. It turned randy. When women would stand by his piano to listen to his playing (which they did less and less these days) it would try and force itself down their tops or up their skirts. These women (who were proper and often fancied themselves as upper class) were horrified by the hand's behavior and would blame it on him. The hand was slapped, but so was he – in the face. It was no use trying to explain that he was not responsible for the hand's habits. It was connected to him, and so the ladies' reasoned, it *was* him!

The manager took him to one side.
"Listen. These antics cannot continue. I've been turning a blind eye up until now because I knew that you needed a job. However, it is up to me to run a respectable ship. There are rules to be followed. Your wild playing is way out of line. And as for your recent ways with the women....I am going to have to let you go. Without notice."
The hand grabbed the manager by the throat and squeezed. The pianist was horrified. Was the hand capable of murder? He tried to will it to let go but it only tightened its grip. The manager started turning red in the face and struggling for breath. The pianist began to panic, his stomach churning. What would be the consequences of this? Would charges be pressed?
Finally, the hand released its grip. The blood drained out of the strangled man's throat.
"Right that's it. You're leaving at the next port. We're calling in at Sydney tomorrow. You're to stay in your cabin until then. I don't want you roaming the ship. You're dangerous. You're lucky I'm not calling the police."

Back in his cabin, the pianist mused on recent events. The hand had got him into trouble, *deep* trouble. He wanted to return it to the manufacturer. He wanted his money back. There was nothing for it – he would have to return it to where it had come from and ask for a refund. He should have known it was too good to be true – an all singing, all dancing hand that could play the piano in an accomplished manner. A hand that could play as competently as a real human hand. The hand was possessed.

He had purchased the hand from the suburbs of Sydney, in Darlington, in an old disused warehouse that had been converted. It had been manufactured by a bunch of ex-programmers who had banded together, having left their former companies. He should have known better than to buy it on the black market.

He disembarked at Sydney, went home to his flat in Newtown and the next day, took a bus out to where the warehouse was located. Old newspapers were blown down the street by the wind and a few mangy looking cats roamed around. Seeing the warehouse up ahead of him, he did not take the front entrance. Instead he snuck in around the back and had a good snoop around. There were several large television screens mounted upon the walls. On the TV screens were displayed a number of amputees making fools of themselves; joggers running backwards, ballet dancers doing the highland fling, skiers crashing into other skiers. He was so engrossed in the action that he did not notice that somebody else had entered the room. Suddenly the screens were switched off, went blank.

"Well what have we here then? Bit of a nosey parker, is it?"

The pianist froze. Busted. A man with a glass eye walked into his field of vision.

"Thought you'd come and see what was what, did you?" he said in an extremely intimidating manner.

He wore a long black overcoat and walked with a cane. The pianist gathered his courage.

"All these people on the screens. They're all amputees that you're meant to be helping. But you're ruining their lives. You're selling them faulty limbs and so they're making idiots of themselves in public. You're ruining careers. It's not fair. You need to stop it. Right now. It's evil, pure evil."

The man with the glass eye laughed.

"The world *is* evil", he said. "Anybody who claims otherwise is a naïve idiot. We've all been hard done by. We've all been fired from our jobs – without redundancy packages I might add. Severance without pay. This is what you get when programmers go to the dark side. This is what you get when global corporations don't treat people right. Surveillance cameras are fitted into the prosthetic limbs so we back here at base can have a good laugh."

The pianist couldn't help himself. A sob escaped his lips.

"*How could you?*" he shouted. "How could you take it out on defenseless amputees? Those people are already down on their luck. They've lost a limb and often their livelihood with it. What you've done is the lowest of the low."

The head developer looked ashamed.

"What about what happened to *me?* What about how *I* was treated?"

"You shouldn't abuse other people just because you've been mistreated. I know it's hard but you need to try and rise above the harsh blows. To absorb them somehow without giving hatred back. You're obviously very talented. Can't you put your talents to use for good rather than evil?"

There was a lengthy pause.

"I'll leave you with that thought", said the pianist and left the building.

The pianist returned to his rented accommodation. How the hell was he going to survive without the money that playing on the cruise ships brought in? There were other more serious considerations too. The hand had stopped obeying him when he was eating. It would play up, play silly buggers, flick food onto the floor and onto the far wall, treating his eating like a game. He had got around this problem by using his other arm (thank God he hadn't lost both to gangrene!). He was right-handed so everything was awkward, but then everything *had* been awkward since losing his arm. Food preparation was also a problem – he could no longer use the prosthetic arm for this as it would go crazy with the knives and attempt to chop at his good hand.

He had been at home for five days when things started to come right. He was eating his morning muesli and decided to give the prosthetic hand a tentative try with the milk pouring. Miraculously, it obeyed! The milk did not spill over onto the table as he had feared that it might, instead it flowed smoothly into his bowl. He decided to give the arm a go with the spoon. He shifted the silver implement from his left hand into his right and focused hard on sending the correct signals from his brain to his residual limb. More success! The spoon rose effortlessly to his mouth – the food was delivered, chewed and digested.

In the past, the hand had not complied when he was dressing. Today, it behaved perfectly, doing up the buttons on his shirt and zipping up his fly, pulling on his socks and tying the laces on his shoes. It was nothing short of a miracle.

The next day there was an article in the Sydney Morning Herald.

Police were pleasantly surprised today when they went to investigate suspicious happenings in a warehouse in Darlington. Tipped off by an amputee who wishes to remain anonymous, the police were seeking to arrest Andrew Edwards, and were seeking evidence that he had been controlling prosthetic limbs remotely and in a malicious manner, seeking to harm others. However, when they arrived at the warehouse from which Mr Edwards and his colleagues work, Mr Edwards confessed that although he had been remotely controlling the limbs in the past he had now seen the error of his ways and that the prosthetic limbs were now fully controlled by the amputee's brains. Mr Edwards had assured police that he has now disabled the capability for the software to be controlled remotely. Over ten amputees have filed claims against Mr Edwards, but they are now reporting that their limbs are working properly again. No charges will be pressed but several of the victims are seeking damages.

The pianist filed for damages and was awarded $30,000 for loss of earnings. Several weeks after the money arrived in his bank account a small newspaper clipping arrived in the post.

Pianist wanted for cabaret bar.
Must be able to work evenings and weekends.
 Tel. 9651 2455

The initials A.E. were penned in the right hand corner of the clipping with the words 'good luck' written afterwards.

Vision

Gary was working in his dark room when the stroke took place. There was nobody with him but he knew enough to know that something was terribly wrong as his balance felt suddenly off and his left arm had become uncomfortably numb. He made his way into the living room and dialled 111. The ambulance arrived shortly afterwards and he was taken to A&E and triaged. The doctor, who looked half Gary's age, diagnosed a stroke and Gary was kept in for observation as his blood pressure was 200 over 90, no doubt a contributing factor to what he had suffered. They gave him medication for the blood pressure and let him go home after three days. He no longer saw colour; his world had become black and white. The doctor told him that the stroke had done damage to his occipital lobe.

Gary lived alone in Point Chev. His wife had committed suicide a year earlier and he had fallen into a deep depression. He had no interest in other women. Gary didn't know why his wife had suicided, but he knew she had always complained that he was too wrapped up in his work and never seemed to have any time for her, so he felt a requisite amount of guilt. Following the death of his wife, Gary managed to continue with his photography but it was an effort, like wading through glue. He was well respected in his profession and had held a number of successful exhibitions. He knew he was one of the lucky ones; he made a living from his art, a rare and difficult feat in small, isolated New Zealand. People called him egotistical but it was just a defence mechanism, a way of keeping his psyche intact when he was picked at and criticised. He didn't have too many friends. People said he was 'difficult'. He spent most of his time holed up in his dark room, fiddling with chemicals, watching photographs appear in the developing solution.

He joined the stroke foundation because he thought that he should. They offered him little in the way of comfort – just an online support group and a monthly newsletter. He always read the newsletter. He found his new existence rather restricted. He could no longer develop colour photographs and so was forced to do black and white pictures only. Managing around the house became more of a struggle. The stroke had rendered his left arm partially paralysed and finding the right words to say often took longer than it used to. Matching thoughts to words was difficult. Everything seemed a strain. Making a cup of tea was as hard as climbing Everest.

When the stroke foundation contacted him to do a colour brochure for them his initial impulse was to say no. How could he possibly work in colour now? It was Gary's neighbour who suggested hiring an apprentice – somebody to help out, somebody whose vision was completely intact. Gary advertised in the local rag.
    WANTED
Apprentice photographer to work in colour.
Must have meticulous attention to detail.

And beneath that his phone number. He wasn't exactly inundated with calls, but three days after Gary had placed the ad Philip rang and expressed his interest in the position. Gary invited him to the house for an interview. He seemed personable enough and brought with him an impressive portfolio of work. Gary told him about the brochure he had been asked to produce and Philip showed an appropriate amount of interest. Gary felt strongly about doing the brochure that had been requested. After all, was it not a cause close to his heart? After the interview, Gary rang Philip's referees and they spoke very highly of him. One was an established photographer that Gary knew of, the other was a gallery owner who ran a large gallery in downtown Auckland.

Gary phoned Philip and asked him to come over on Monday. Philip did as he was asked. The older man had been out over the weekend photographing healthy looking people doing healthy activities which was what the Stroke Foundation had asked for.
"I've been to Photograph School at the New York Film Academy you know", boasted Philip as he removed one of the photos from the fixer.
"Well la di bloody da", said Gary. "There was no fancy schmancy Photoshop when I learned the tricks of my trade. Still, do well on this project and there could well be other work in the pipeline for you."
"Photoshop's old hat now. You should get with the program buddy."
Buddy, Gary cringed when he heard the word.
Philip pulled his MacBook Pro from his backpack.
"You need to learn to master a photo editing suite."
I'm not your bloody buddy, he thought. I've only known you five minutes, furthermore I'm your <u>employer</u> not your friend. And what was a suite anyway?
The only suites that Gary knew were lounge suites.

Philip was a fast worker and the job was finished in no time at all. Philip had to do most of his work with Gary hovering behind him, nit-picking.

"Why are you making that lady's nose smaller? Why don't you give that man rosier looking cheeks? These are meant to be fit looking people you know. People who *haven't* had nor are ever likely to have a stroke. These are the people to aspire to."

Philip ignored most of what Gary said. After all, what formal education had Gary ever had? Everybody who was anybody knew that he was self taught, one of the Established most definitely with a capital 'E'. Gary liked to boast in public that he had come up the hard way, via the school of hard knocks and had disdained any photographic training.

When the work was done Gary emailed the stroke foundation taking full credit for the work, stating that he didn't want any payment and not mentioning Philip's name. Philip read the email in Gary's Sent Mail when Gary wasn't looking. He was furious. He confronted Gary the next morning over the phone.

"How come *I* don't get any of the credit?"

"How do you know whether or not you got credit? Been reading my emails have you? Nosy parker. You should learn to mind your own business. Snooping will only bring you trouble. I'm the one that did the bulk of the work, the hard graft. All you did was fart arse about on your computer. It's *my* name and my name only that should be printed in the brochure."

"Right", thought Philip. "I'll teach you what's what."

He turned all the work purple in Photoshop and sent it in to the Stroke Foundation who loved the new changes. He also sent in his name as Chief Assistant. The photos were published in the new purple shade with the credits and people loved it.

"So fresh, original and modern", they cooed.

Philip lapped up the praise and now it was Gary's turn for fury.

"I wish I'd never hired a bloody assistant", he bellowed when Philip showed up at his house with his bank account details. "Why did *I* have to have a stroke – why me?"

It was a plaintiff question for which there was no answer. Only God if there was one knew the reason and he was keeping mum.

"You're fired" he said. "I knew it was a mistake to stop working solo. It could only lead to trouble."

"Fine", said Philip. "I'll leave as soon as I've got my money."

Gary took fifty dollars from his wallet and put it down upon the table.

"Fifty bucks! Fifty measly bucks! That's not what we agreed."

"Well, what did we agree?"

"Five hundred."

"Five bloody hundred! Get off the grass. You've got to be joking. Do you think I'm stupid as well as old and lame! Think the stroke's damaged my cognition do you? Well I've still got my wits about me.

We don't even have a contract so you don't have a leg to stand on. Sixty's my highest offer, take it or leave it."

He slammed another ten dollars down upon the table.

"Stingy miser, aren't you?" asked Philip rhetorically, snatching up the money. "Sixty bucks is an insult, I wish I'd never answered your stupid ad, I wish I'd never even met you."

"The feeling's mutual *buddy*, believe me, the feeling's mutual."

Philip exited the room, slamming the door behind him and the two men never spoke nor met again.

Marsha's Deal

The Reckoning

Marsha Lee Henry died on a Friday. She took her own life at Dignitas, the Swiss euthanasia clinic, after being diagnosed with Fibrodysplasia ossificans progressiva, a rare disease that meant various parts of her body would turn to bone when damaged. She was beyond finding Dignitas creepy; she simply wanted to die. Enough was enough. She'd taken years of it, years of her body slowly turning to bone, trapping her, encasing her. She may as well have been turning to stone, like somebody who had looked into Medusa's eyes. She had filled out the Dignitas forms at home, passed their tests and been accepted. She had won the right to end her own life.

She had made the journey solo; a lonely trip. She had thought at the time that it was a one way ticket to the grave but this did not turn out to be the case. Her body was cremated; her spirit went straight to hell. She found herself face to face with the Devil. "Hello there", said the Devil. "I've been expecting you."

Marsha knew that the Devil, like God, was omniscient, so she kept silent. She looked around, taking in her surroundings. The environment was made of hard concrete with not much in the way of luxury. There were several steel planks to sit on, and three large TV screens hooked up to DVD players. Puffs of smoke wafted out from behind them. Nobody else was around. Marsha was horribly, terribly alone. She looked down at her body. At least one of her wishes had been granted – she was no longer a woman of bone; she had turned back to flesh. It had been years since she had been flexible and she did a few stretches, testing out her new suppleness.

"Fancy a steam bath?", asked the Devil, gesturing towards the wisps of smoke.

Marsha breathed deeply into both nostrils and drew courage. She did not tremble, she did not quake.

"Actually", she said. "What I *would* like is another crack at it."

"Crack at what?"

"At *life*."

"What on earth do you mean?"

"I would like to be reborn as a baby, as myself. I want my time again, a second chance. This time around I don't want to be afflicted by disease. I want a clean life, a good life, a life of joy and happiness."

"You *yourself* are responsible for creating an awful lot of sorrow", said the Devil in a menacing tone, with a twitch of his horns. "Would you like to have a look at some of the misery you've left behind?"

Marsha hesitated. She knew that her absence must have left a void in a few hearts and minds and she felt no small amount of guilt. Suicide was selfish, wasn't that what they said. Was it true? Was it accurate even in the case of somebody diagnosed with a life threatening, life altering, illness?

"Okay then", said Marsha. "Show me the worst."

The Devil picked up a DVD remote, pressed play and said "Now I will show you those left behind."

The sobbing form of Marsha's husband started playing and Marsha felt a pang of sorrow shoot through her. What had she done? What fresh misery was this? Don was her one true love, her reason for existing, but he hadn't wanted her to go to Dignitas; she'd stolen away behind his back and look (*just look!*) at the grief it had caused. Don was beside himself, lying distraught on the sofa while great sobs wracked his body. Moving pictures of her friends were next; Bettie, one of her fellow seamstresses and Lucille, her old friend from high school, both of them overwhelmed with quiet despair. Most heartbreakingly of all, footage of her daughter Ingrid was shown, alone in her Christchurch bedsit, clutching a photo of her adoptive mother and sobbing into her pillow. The only person who'd known about her trip to Dignitas was her sister, her brilliant sister, by now an IT consultant in Auckland, who'd come up with the money when Marsha had phoned and confronted her with her exit plans and her reason for them. Overcome by the footage, Marsha turned to The Devil and apologised.

"I'm sorry", she said. "I'm sorry for all the things I've done wrong, the bad decisions and the faulty moves. If you just give me one more chance at rebirth, I promise you I'll make you a better job of it. I'll right my wrongs. I'll fix my mistakes. I'll be a model citizen. I'll never do any harm."

"Your race has already been run," said The Devil. "What makes you think that *you* deserve a second chance?"

"I wish I'd known at the start what I know now."

The Devil scoffed.

"That's what they all say", he said. "All new entrants to hell get shown a retrospective."

He gestured towards a hard steel plank and Marsha obediently took a seat.

"So without further adieu," boomed The Devil. "Marsha Lee Henry. This is your life!"
He pressed play on a DVD remote.

Marsha watched her life being played out before her very eyes, bore witness to her birth, saw herself playing with a mobile hung high above her cot, observed her first tentative steps, then onwards towards kindergarten and primary school, where she played elastics and knucklebones. Then to intermediate, where she held hands with her first boyfriend and received her first telling off from the school headmistress for losing her red parka and having to collect it after assembly. She won the standard two cross country, much to her mother's disbelief *'that can't be my child crossing the finish line in first place'*, the bitchy school girl games that start up early, then high school with its peer pressure and politics. Her family, through it all, in the background, her mother a social worker, working with kids from problem families, her dad a humble electrician, often out of work and her over achieving sister Natalie, top of her class in mathematics and English and a local ballet star, regularly performing at the local theatre. A show off to Marsha's mind, but then Marsha was no great shakes at anything scholastic, although she was a whiz behind the sewing machine and had been given an old Singer for her birthday on which she had run up frocks for herself, Natalie and her mother, two barbecue aprons for her Dad and various outfits for the family cat. Leaving school at fifteen, the earliest age possible, and becoming a seamstress seemed like a natural choice. Marsha took work in a local factory, apprenticed to Lucinda Bragglethwaite. And then the disease had set in.

An image of one of her old school friends came up on the DVD. Linda Davidson, who had been with her through high school, a constant companion, there in times of trouble, with Marsha through thick and thin. Linda was a firm friend, a person you could rely on. She hadn't turned away when Marsha had started turning to bone. A friend in need; a friend indeed.
"Hey", said Marsha. "What's Linda doing inserted there in the DVD just randomly like that?"
"Blast from the past, eh?" mocked the Devil with a cackle. "She's dead now. Got hit by a truck driving home from work one day. If you stick around I can re-introduce the two of you."
He paused.
"Why do you want to go back to earth anyway? It's much nicer down here."

He winked, then waltzed over to Marsha and coyly put one arm around her shoulders.

"Stay with me Marsha. Stay and be my companion. Stay and keep me company. Stay and be my friend. Stay and be *more* than just a friend, if you get my gist."

He got down on one knee.

"Life is rotten on Planet Earth, Marsha. War, violence, famine, rape, murder. There's none of that carry on down here. Just me and my...cronies. I can show you a good time. I can make your dreams come true. I can give you a warm place to sleep at night. You'll never want for anything again if you just say you'll stay with me, yes stay."

For a moment Marsha forgot herself, staring into the Devil's eyes, as he wooed her with his promises, then she jumped back to her senses with a start remembering where she was and who she was and who *He* was.

"I'm sorry", she said (her mother had trained her to always be polite, even in the most trying of circumstances), "but I just don't believe a word you say. I ask you for just one thing. To go back to earth as a baby and to have a chance to live my life over again, and this time I don't want to be afflicted with Fibrodysplasia ossificans progressiva thank *you* very much."

She smiled at the Devil and He grinned back.

"Please good Sir," she added as an afterthought.

"Oh alright then, since you asked so nicely", said Satan. "Besides, I've been waiting for a new project to come along. You'll have to pay me of course."

"Pay you?"

Marsha looked around for her purse.

"Pay you how?"

The devil tapped his nose with one finger.

"That's for me to know and for you to find out, sunshine."

He picked up his long pointy tail and swung it around in the air several times. Marsha felt like asking him what the hell he was doing, but she kept silent, hoping that he knew his stuff when it came to terrestrial transportation.

"Marsha Lee Henry I declare you reborn!"

He reached out and touched Marsha's shoulders. Marsha felt herself becoming lighter and lighter, felt her spirit detach itself from her body, keeping her mind. She grew faint and more and more distant and then the next thing she knew she was reborn.

The First Time Around

The Blue Man Pub was Marsha's local watering hole, and she could often be found there on a Friday, after work with two or three of her seamstress friends. They were underage drinkers. They were only sixteen but they looked older and the barman did not press them for ID. Marsha's condition had only just begun to manifest and had not yet been diagnosed, so she herself did not fully understand why she struggled to raise her arms up high enough to brush her hair and why dressing had become such a struggle. She was a stoic girl and she did not like to make a fuss. The bar was located in central Wellington, the prices were affordable and the beer and wine were pleasant. It was here that Marsha first met Don. The jukebox played in the background. Don, who was covered in sawdust, saw Marsha sitting with a group of her seamstress friends at a table on the other side of the bar, caught her eye and winked. Marsha blushed. She hadn't had much experience with men and she wasn't sure what to do. Should she look the other way? Should she wink back? She liked the look of Don, who was rugged and handsome, fit and strong from his building work and from playing rugby twice a week. She giggled, took a sip of her drink and coyly looked away. Don, who had only marginally more experience with women than Marsha had with men, turned to his friend Harry and said "Hey Harry, I like the look of that girl over there. The one in the red flowery dress. What do you think I should do?"
"Buy her a drink, you idiot. That's the best way to break the ice."
Harry looked over at the table where Marsha was sitting.
"Get her a white wine. That's what she's drinking."
Don ordered a white wine and walked with it, trembling, over to where Marsha sat.
"Oh, hello there", he said. "You caught my eye. I bought you a white wine."
Marsha giggled again, then reached out and took the glass of wine, brushing Don's fingers with her own as she did so.
"Thank you very much", she said, taking the glass of wine from his hand.
She gestured at the empty seat next to her own.
"Please, take a seat."
Don sat. Marsha took a small, lady-like sip of her wine, then a larger drink and then, much to Don's amazement, picked up the wine glass and drained the entire contents. Don looked astounded.

"Gosh", he said. "I've never seen a woman drink like *that* before."
Marsha smacked her lips.
"Down the hatch", she said. "Dutch courage."
And she rose to her feet and gave Don a kiss full on the lips *muack* just like that. It was Don's turn to blush. His mate, Harry, over at the bar, gave a cheer.
"Looks like you're in there, chum", he hollered, and gave a thumbs up.
And so the relationship was born.

***

Shortly after her sixteenth birthday, Marsha tripped over the corner of a rug in her home and hit her hip on the corner of a table. It bruised and a second bone grew and Marsha began to have difficulty walking. Her family couldn't help but notice and her mother took her to the doctor who referred them to a specialist. After a series of tests, Fibrodysplasia ossificans progressiva, one of the world's rarest conditions was diagnosed. Marsha and her mother were at a loss as to what to do. Marsha's mother did not want Marsha to know what lay in store for her; she wanted to protect her child, so she did not quiz the specialist in front of Marsha. Instead, she waited until they got home and then made a private phone call.

"Hello, it's just Isobel Williams here, calling about my daughter Marsha. We were in to see you earlier today. I was just wondering what we can expect as this…infirmity progresses."

"I'll be perfectly frank with you Isobel, it's not going to be pretty. Marsha will become gradually trapped in a second skeleton. She will find it more and more difficult to move and may have difficulty eating and swallowing. It is likely that she will be bedridden by thirty and dead by forty."

"So her body will make extra bone constantly."

"No. She may go months without a flare-up and then the disease can start up again. Nobody knows why. This can happen spontaneously but is likely to happen if she damages herself say through a fall, muscle overexertion, an injury, injection, surgery or even a virus."

"I see. Is there anything we can do to slow or halt the progress of this terrible condition?"

"I'm sorry, no. It's a genetic disorder. Marsha has just been extremely unlucky. She's been thrown a curve ball, dealt a bad card."

"Oh well, that's life", said Isobel, doing her best to take a stiff upper lip approach. "We shall simply solider on. Thank you very much for your time doctor."

She put down the phone and burst into floods of tears.

***

The quarter acre section in Lower Hutt was selling cheap. Not for the first time, Don's profession came in handy and he was able to build their house himself, a labour of love, a three bedroom weatherboard A frame number with aluminium windows. Don and Marsha moved in together when they were in their early twenties. They were in love, arguments were rare and they cohabited happily together. Marsha had been frank with Don about her medical condition and he was aware that as it progressed he might have to become her caregiver. She already had difficulty walking due to the fact that she had banged her hip, but she got around by swinging one leg out wide as she went. They were frighteningly traditional. Don paid the bills; Marsha cooked the meals and took care of the housework. She did not complain much about her condition. Her mother had sheltered her from full knowledge, but she had been to the library and found an encyclopaedia article on the disorder so she knew some of what lay in store for her.

Unrelated but additional to Marsha's condition, there were fertility problems. They tried and they tried but they could not conceive. Unsure as to whether the problem lay with Don or Marsha the two of them went together to the family doctor. Don provided semen for analysis, booked in for a testicular biopsy and had a blood test to determine his testosterone level. Marsha had ovulation and ovarian reserve testing and an X-Ray of her uterus. The results came back. They both had issues. Don's sperm weren't swimming and Marsha's eggs were not maturing as they should.

They decided to adopt. Together they visited Orlando's Orphanage. The orphanage was run by a strict matron who went by the name of Mrs Hamble. Don and Marsha walked together down the aisles of cots, peering into half-starved sleeping faces, trying to decide who to pick. There were differences of opinion. Don liked the look of this one, Marsha liked the look of that one - it was difficult for them to reach consensus. Most of the kids were crying and had snot running down their faces. At the end of one row, in a cot with one of the sides down lay a child who did not cry, a child who did not scream. This held instant appeal for Marsha, who wanted an easy baby, not somebody who was going to shout the house down. They had a spare room. They could accommodate it. Financially it might be a bit of a struggle, but nothing they couldn't take. At that very moment, at that point in time, there was nothing that Marsha Lee Henry wanted more in the world than to take home an adopted child. But not just any old kid. She wanted a specific sprog, the one in the cot in front of her, the quiet one, the one who did not kick and scream and make a fuss, the one who, although only an infant, knew how to behave itself, knew how to conduct herself in this wicked, terrible, wonderful world.

Marsha leaned over and picked up the baby. It smiled up at her with her blue eyes. It gurgled a bit and cooed. Marsha cuddled it closer, wrapping its shawl more tightly around it to keep out the cold and then handed it to Don. Don didn't quite know what to do with it, but at Marsha's prompting he gave it a snuggle and then he too was smitten. Mrs Hamble was standing in the doorway with her hand on her hip.

"Well", she said. "Do you want the baby or not?"

Marsha, who dreaded to think about the abuse that might go on within the four walls of this terrible place, quickly nodded. Marsha named the baby Ingrid in her mind. Still carrying the baby, they made their way to Mrs Hamble's office. Everything inside was orderly and efficient. Money (quite a lot of it, to Marsha's thinking) was exchanged. Papers were signed. And the baby, the baby, was theirs.

"A baby!" exclaimed Marsha to Don when they had exited the horrible institution and were outside in the safety of their car. "Just imagine, a baby!"

A baby to have, a baby to hold. A baby to nurture and attend to, a baby to feed and to rock to sleep at night. A baby to sing sweet lullabies to and to soothe when it woke, crying, from nightmares. Somebody else's baby actually, an unwanted child, a baby that somebody else had, freely, given away. Marsha couldn't imagine why anybody would give away something as precious as a child. Was this child the result of an unwanted pregnancy? Was this baby, heaven forbid, the product of rape? She looked down at the tiny face, wrapped up in its white orphanage blanket, a blanket that was covered in stains. Why on *earth* would anybody give this baby away? No room at the inn perhaps. No money. Money too tight to mention. She cuddled the baby closer, then stared out the window at the cold dark night, lit only by a few dull stars. It was a cold world, and cruel, thought Marsha. Everything boiled down to money in the end. The root of all things dark and evil. Whatever happened to kindness and compassion?

They took the baby home, gave it a bottle of formula milk which they had bought in preparation and tucked it into the cot with the pink fluffy blanket covered in ABC lettering that Marsha had picked up cheap from the charity store. She sucked her thumb and settled into sleep, just as if she had always lived with Don and Marsha, in this home, in this street, in this particular suburb, on this island in the South Pacific in this corner of the globe. Marsha looked down at the quietly sleeping form and said

"*Ingrid.* Let's call her Ingrid." Don nodded in agreement. They both left the room.

Don and Marsha loved Ingrid unconditionally, just as surely as if she were their own child. Marsha bought her dolls from money she had saved working as a seamstress and Don built her a playhouse for the dolls to play in. He also built her a hut in a fig tree in the backyard, a swing and, when she was a little older, a wooden go-cart for her fifth birthday. Ingrid, who had been rather unceremoniously dumped on the doorstep of the nearest orphanage when she was two days old, latched onto the warmth and affection now offered her like a limpet clasping onto a rock. There seemed no prospect of her ever letting go. Ingrid grew quickly and soon Marsha was enrolling her at Chilton James Primary School, where took a special shine to Miss Sampson, a kindly soul who always let Ingrid play for extra time in the sandpit and encouraged her in singing and colour painting.

During these primary school painting sessions, Ingrid made many vibrant, joyful depictions of her home life; pictures of Marsha pulling a fresh tray of scones from the oven, drawings of Don knocking up a garden shed from old bits of four by two that had been lying around the house. She also drew sketches of Marsha at her Singer sewing machine, running up Ingrid's outfits; trousers and shirts and skirts. Miss Sampson always praised these paintings, glorified them to the high heavens, which of course made the other infants jealous, envy being one of the most primitive emotions and evident even in very small children. Yes, Ingrid may have been Miss Sampson's favourite but this very fact didn't make for an easy life. Because of it, she was picked on and bullied. The other kids threw sand into her eyes in the sandpit, they hit her with sticks and they gave her Chinese burns and snake bites. Miss Sampson would always race to Ingrid's aid which only made things worse in the long run.

When Ingrid told Marsha about the bullying, Marsha was beside herself. She asked Ingrid for the names of the bullies and Ingrid told her. To Marsha's disappointment, Don took a harsh stance.
"It's life in New Zealand", he declared. "Cold and abusive. Being singled out for special treatment means everybody else hates you. The sooner she gets used to that sort of environment the better."
Marsha couldn't believe what Don was saying, yet she knew in her heart of hearts that it was true. What could she do to protect her adopted child from such cruelty? Marsha resolved to go along to the primary school and have a word with Miss Sampson to see if she could be made to understand that it might be best to tone down the favouritism in order that the bullying ease off, or preferably, cease altogether.

Until this point in time, Marsha hadn't known that small children could be so cruel. She had thought that sadism was reserved for the Hitlers and Pol Pots of history – crazed leaders who gained power and then inflicted their twisted versions of authoritarianism upon their countries or the world – not young kids at primary school. During her own early school years she hadn't known any such unkindness, but then again, she hadn't been teacher's pet either.

The following Monday, Marsha put on her best trousers and jacket and headed down to the school. She knocked on the door to Miss Sampson's room.
"Come in."
Marsha entered, swinging her leg beside her as she walked. She was used to people staring at her.
Miss Sampson sat behind a wooden desk. She looked friendly and kind, but Marsha knew she was rather unaware of the damage she was inadvertently inflicting on Ingrid's life due to her favouritism.
"I've come about Ingrid", said Marsha.
"Yes, I thought you might have."
"Don't get me wrong. It's kind of you to take her under your wing. However, in favouring her, you make the other kids jealous and they pick on her."
"Oh, do they?"
Marsha couldn't believe Miss Sampson hadn't noticed. She pointed to the "Bullying: Zero Tolerance" poster that was pinned to the far wall.
"I can't have my child treated badly during the day", she said. "Ingrid comes home in floods of tears and now suffers nightmares and cries out in the night."
"Do you know which students were bullying her? What exactly were they doing?"
"It was Harriet Barker, Samuel Davidson and Sally Robertson. They have been giving her Chinese burns, snake bites and throwing sand into her eyes. It's not fair. If there's no solution I'll have to shift her to another school. Perhaps I could have the phone numbers of the mothers."
"That would be a little outside the norm."
Marsha stood her ground.
"This bullying can't continue. I think it best if you don't favour Ingrid so much and I have a chance to speak to the other mothers. Perhaps those mean children have problems in their home lives that need sorting out."
Miss Sampson took out a pen and paper and rather reluctantly jotted down a few numbers.

"Okay then", she said. "I'm sorry that you feel bullying has gone on at my school. Would you like *me* to ring the mothers and talk to them about the situation?"

Marsha stiffened.

"No no", she said. "It's perfectly fine. I can manage the situation. I can stick up for myself and my daughter."

Marsha walked home with the telephone numbers in her pocket. She entered through the front door, sat down in the living room next to the telephone, withdrew the list from her pocket and dialled. The first number she called was picked up after three rings.

"Hello is that Candice Barker?"

"Speaking."

"Hello my name is Marsha Lee Henry. I wanted to talk to you about some of the things that have been happening at Chilton James Primary School."

"Okay."

"My child is being bullied. It appears that your daughter is one of the main culprits."

"I find that very difficult to believe."

"Well, I'm afraid that it's true. Ingrid says she gave her Chinese burns. Not pleasant in anybody's book."

"I am sorry to hear that. Come to think of it, she has been getting a little more aggressive with her brother of late."

The conversation ended.

Marsha called each of the mothers in turn and explained the situation. Some were understanding, some were not. Some listened, others didn't want to know. Three stayed on the line, one hung up. At the end of it, Marsha told herself that at least she'd given it her best shot and if it still didn't work out they'd change schools to one on the other side of town. She took Ingrid to one side, told her what she'd done, explained the situation to her.

"I'm sticking up for you", she said. "Since you're too young to stick up for yourself. With time you'll learn. You'll learn how to give as good as you get, or to dodge and avoid, or ask a superior for help, all according to circumstances, but right now you needed my help, so I've given it to you for free, as a mother rightly should."

Ingrid, who was too young to fully understand, but still got the gist of it, stood still and smiled and nodded. Marsha gave her a bear hug and an encouraging pat on the back and then sent her off to bed. It was Sunday night. Time to sleep; time to forget. Time to hope that all would be well in the morning.

Come Monday, a nervous Ingrid tottered through the gates of Chilton James Primary School, let go of Marsha's hand, with encouragement and walked into her classroom. She took a seat in her usual place. Nobody bothered her before class started. A miracle! She was being left alone, left to her own devices. She pulled her books from her bag – two Dr Seuss numbers; *Oh, the Thinks You Can Think!* And *Oh Say Can You Say?* At playtime she wasn't bothered and they didn't harass her at lunchtime either. Ingrid thought her mother must have worked a magic spell on the class to turn their attitudes around so successfully and she was ever so grateful. That evening, when she went home, she gave her mother a great big kiss on the cheek *smack!* and said "Thanks very much, Mum" and Marsha knew, without having to be told, exactly what Ingrid was talking about.

***

As her disease progressed, sewing became too difficult for Marsha and she said goodbye to Lucinda and the factory, gave up her job and stayed at home during the day, casually attending to the housework and preparing meals. This led to depression and she began drinking during the day, gin and tonics mostly, which lead to further depression until she took to her bed and wouldn't budge from it except for to pour herself another drink. Don was aware of the situation, but wasn't quite sure what to do about it. Up until this point in time Marsha had been a soldier. Fibrodysplasia ossificans progressiva had been her battleground. Don took on the role that he had known, when they first met, he might have to take – that of caregiver. He brought Marsha meals in bed, which she simply picked at. Her jaws had begun to fuse together. He tried to talk her into getting up, into facing the world. She had become too afraid of damaging herself, of further ossification. The bed was a safe place, she reasoned, a cocoon, a haven. A place where no injuries could occur. Don knew she was on a slippery, downwards, agoraphobic slope. He tried to coax her out of her budding alcoholic hiding place but she would not be budged. She took to ordering bottles of gin and tonic online, the empty bottles building up besides the bed.

Two of her friends from the factory visited. They came together, Doris Heywater and Patricia Halwell; they came bearing flowers and a basket of fruit. Ignoring the empty gin bottles, they sat down together on the end of Marsha's bed and kept talking to her until she emerged from beneath the duvet. She looked a fright; her hair was matted and unkempt and hadn't been washed in two weeks. She was in her nightie. Doris and Patricia did not care. They did not mind, they simply talked on, figuring that their stream of chatter would help to lift Marsha out of the doldrums. It worked. Marsha emerged from her squalor and said "Right then, that's enough of that. I'm sick of wallowing." She picked herself up, dusted herself off, had a shower and with the help of Doris, dressed in some of her best clothes and the three women went out to lunch at a nearby café.

***

Ingrid's first boyfriend was Jimmy Hallsworth, who she met at intermediate school. Jimmy was short for his age, with buck teeth and braces, but she liked him anyway. He had a good sense of humour and was always clowning around to make Ingrid laugh. He also did her favours to make her life easier; carrying her textbooks to school for her, lending her pencils when she had forgotten them, offering her a sandwich if she left her lunch at home by accident. Their first kiss was shared (like many first kisses are) behind the school bike sheds as a group of smokers gathered nearby. Minor fireworks went off inside Ingrid's head. She saw small golden stars. Jimmy, a more down to earth sort, rocked back and forth on his heels in mild delight. They were ever so slightly smitten with each other. It was sweet love, first love, a pure and innocent love, love untainted by jealousy or greed. Jimmy bought a small ring from Habitson & Habitson, a local jewellery store and slid it onto Ingrid's finger.

About three months into the relationship, Jimmy began becoming possessive, constantly quizzing Ingrid about where she was going and who she was going there with. Ingrid hated this; it made her feel suffocated, choked, boxed in. Although she was only thirteen she was her own woman, used to living her own life and Jimmy's constant quizzing felt like restrictions he was placing upon her, as if he was trying to limit what she could do and when she could do it. She politely asked Jimmy to 'give her some space' in the parlance of the day, but Jimmy did not back off. Ingrid felt confined, trapped. She tried to tell Jimmy so, but he would not listen.

When they hit the six month mark Ingrid finally got the nerve to dump Jimmy, who promptly and predictably made his first suicide bid by attempting to hang himself from the bedroom light fitting. Ingrid knew this move had been designed to make her feel guilty and she did feel the requisite pang of culpability and remorse, but then she simply told herself the lie that Jimmy had been unstable from the start and that his current downwards spiral had not been her fault.

***

Ingrid grew older and Marsha grew increasingly frail and progressively trapped in bone. Ingrid enrolled at Hutt Valley High School where at first, she was popular with the lads, and a little less so with the ladies due to the green eyed monster rearing its head in her life once again. Being older, Ingrid lived in fear that her mother would march down to the school to sort things out as she had done

31

when she was young (*O the embarrassment!*) She took her mother to one side and had a word and stated that she was not under any circumstances to venture down to the school to fight Ingrid's battles now that Ingrid was older.

"I'm big enough and ugly enough to fight my own wars now Mum", Ingrid stubbornly declared.

Shortly after her thirteenth birthday Ingrid was befriended a group of the more popular girls, led by Bessie Hawkins. They would forge lunch passes and go into town at lunch time to suss out the booty. Bessie was the Queen of the Gang. She never got caught. Unlike some of the others, the novices. She'd give the orders and wait outside the shop, nonchalantly looking at her nails. She'd wait for the other girls to do their pilfering (lipsticks, mascaras, expensive perfumes, scarves, the odd handbag) then pile the lot into her empty schoolbag, to be sold to the highest bidder at that afternoon's four o'clock auction held behind the school bike sheds. Nobody messed with Bessie. Ingrid felt privileged to be part of a gang; she was just new to the school and had not yet made any other real friends. There was a real excitement to be had from hanging around with the wrong crowd so she didn't bother too much about the consequences.

After two or three sessions as an apprentice Ingrid was now on her own with a list of items that she had to procure. She went into Wellington on a Friday night, telling her mother that she was buying a birthday present for her friend. After catching the bus into town she met up with Bessie and two of the other girls. After an initial briefing they decided to split up and meet back at the bus station in two hours time. After an hour's effort, Ingrid was feeling confident. She had managed to procure most of the items on Bessie's list and was about to head back when she saw out of the corner of her eye a pair of gorgeous Jimmy Choo shoes in a shopping mall just begging to be taken, $1200 price tag and all. Ingrid couldn't resist. *Why not?* she thought. After all, she was flying high, on a roll; she had really mastered this art. She unobtrusively picked up the shoes and put them in her handbag, then waltzed casually out the door.

Just as she stepped through the doorway, a firm hand came down upon her shoulder.

"Hello there Miss. Would you please accompany me back into the store?"

Ingrid felt sick to her stomach. Her mind raced. What the hell was she going to say? What on earth could be her excuse? She was taken by the arm upstairs into an office where they proceeded to ring the police. Shortly after the plain clothes detectives arrived and started questioning her. He also asked her to empty out all the contents of her bag on the table. There lay the incriminating Jimmy Choos along with Bessie's booty. Ingrid, who was a good girl at heart, was petrified.

"What have you got to say for yourself?" asked the detective.

"I'm sorry", she said. "I just fell in with a bad crowd for a short while. I haven't even known them that long. I thought they seemed okay at first, then they got into shop-lifting. I just went along with the flow. I'm not the ringleader, honest."

She froze. Had she said too much?

"So, who is the ringleader of this little racket then?"

"Sorry I can't say. I've said to much already."

"Right then. Like that is it. This is a serious offence, missy. We're going to have to refer you to Child, Youth and Family. We'll take you home and talk to your parents."

Ingrid was swiftly escorted to the detective's Mondeo and they sped off in the direction of Ingrid's home. Marsha was just finishing cooking the dinner when the door opened and Ingrid appeared with the shadow of the detective behind her. Marsha peered out into the evening gloom, trying to see who was accompanying her daughter. Was it a new boyfriend? No, too old for that. The detective stepped forward into the light.

"Good evening Mrs Henry. I'm Detective Sargent Craigson. I'm afraid to tell you that your daughter was apprehended shop-lifting in a Wellington mall this afternoon and she had over $1500 worth of goods on her."

Marsha's hand flew up to her face.

"Oh my", she said. "Oh Ingrid what's been going on? This isn't like you."

Ingrid burst into tears.

"I'm sorry Mum. I just went along with the others. I just wanted to fit in."

"So what's going to happen now?" Marsha asked the detective.

"She will be referred to Youth Justice for Child, Youth and Family. A family group conference will be called which will involve the parents, the school, her family, social worker and the police. This will be a preventative measure to make sure this kind of thing never happens again. She may also be banned from that mall for a specific period of time. We would also like to dissuade her from hanging around with the same group of people. We will be visiting the school to find out who the others were."

Ingrid slumped into the chair, head in hands. She'd been on such a high, invincible, the incredible thieving woman and now she lay in ruins about to take the others down with her, unbeknown to them.

The following Monday Ingrid, filled with dread, tried to get out of going to school, but Marsha wasn't wearing a bar of it.
"You'll face up to your misdemeanours", she said. "It's part of being an adult. You'll thank me for it one day."
Yeah right, muttered Ingrid under her breath.
She packed her bag and, with a sick feeling in her stomach, caught the bus to school and wished for a cloak of invisibility. She entered the classroom and Bessie was the first one she saw. Bessie beckoned her over.
"What happened to you on Friday night then?"
Ingrid wished the ground would open up and swallow her whole. She decided that the best course of action was to confess.
"Look" she said. "I got caught shop-lifting at the mall and was taken home by the cops."
Bessie's face clouded over, then became hard.
"You'd better not have dobbed me in otherwise watch yer back."
The morning bell rung, for which Ingrid was thankful, and she scurried to her desk.

She spent the rest of the day avoiding Bessie but knew that sooner or later she would have to face the inevitable. She was walking to the bus at the end of the day when she saw Bessie and a couple of the other girls loitering by the school gate, smoking. She tried to walk past them with her head down but one of them pushed her into a nearby hedge.
"Been dobbing us in eh? Should've known you were too good to be true."
"New to the gang and not to be trusted", chimed in another.
"That bloody detective was on my case because of you", said Bessie. "Should've kept your big trap shut."
Ingrid said nothing – to speak up in her own self defence seemed futile.
"You better keep out of our way in future, we don't want narks like you hanging around."

Shaken, Ingrid headed for the safety of the school bus, breathing a sigh of relief as she climbed the stairs.

***

Don became Marsha's caregiver. He took on the role willingly and did not act begrudgingly towards her. Marsha became more

34

unstable and unsteady on her feet and falls became increasingly common which lead to further damage and bone growth. It was a vicious cycle she was trapped in. However, she continued to face the world with bravery and did not take to her bed or the bottle again. Marsha couldn't cook or clean anymore, but she read a lot; from Byron to Bronte, from Bukowski to Barnes, she took to devouring books with a vengeance and Don was glad that she was still improving her mind as her body quickly deteriorated. Her friends from the factory proved themselves to be true and visited her once a week, often bringing home baking or flowers to cheer her up. If it was not for this, hers would have been an isolated, solitary existence, shut away from the world and locked up in bone, her face turned away from the sun, inclined towards the pages of a book. She was losing herself in literature. Like many before her, she was seeking solace in words when the world, and her own body, had let her down so badly.

***

The remainder of Ingrid's high school years passed without remarkable event. She was a good student who brought home good marks. She kept Marsha and Don happy. She did not steal again. Shortly after her twentieth birthday, Ingrid made up her mind to find out who her real mother was. She made her way to the nearest Child, Youth and Family office and asked for information about her natural mother. She was given the name Jenny Robinson and a phone number. Ingrid returned home and, with trembling hands, phoned her real mother. The telephone was picked up after three rings.

"Hello."

There was a hint of hardness in the voice, a rough voice, a voice that had been around the block a couple of times. Ingrid was unsure of what she should say – she found herself wishing that she had rehearsed her lines before calling.

"Hello", she said. "My name is Ingrid Anderson. I believe you are my mother."

There was a long pause and then the voice quietly said, "I did give a baby up for adoption some twenty year ago yes. I'm glad you've tracked me down. I've spent a long time wondering what had become of you."

And she promptly burst into tears.

Ingrid hesitated. What she felt like saying was, *but you didn't try and track me down, did you?* but she knew that there may have been complicating factors, laws around tracking down adopted children.

"So, do you have a partner?"

"Yes. I live with John. A zookeeper at the Auckland zoo. How about you?"

"No, I'm single."

"It's good to hear your voice after all these years."

"How old were you when you had me?"

"I was only fifteen. It was just a quick fling out the back of the movie theatre where I worked as an usher. I was in no financial position to be keeping a baby. Please try and understand love. Don't take it personally."

"I have to go", said Ingrid, suddenly overcome with emotion. "I'll see you later."

She hung up the phone without waiting for Jenny to say goodbye.

Ingrid did not want to arrange a meeting with her adopted mother. Part of her was angry, furious even, that she had been given away. Surely Jenny could have found a way to keep her, lived at home with her mother for a while longer, possibly, or gone on some kind of benefit. She had been given up too easily, thought Ingrid. Jenny hadn't valued her highly enough.

***

As she grew increasingly encased in bone, Marsha did not want to be a burden to her family. She went online and filled out the forms to suicide at Dignitas. The contract was signed. She telephoned her sister to advise her of her plans and to ask her for money. She bought her plane ticket to Switzerland. She kept her date with Nembutal, she kept her date with death.

***

The Second Time Around

Marsha was reborn in the maternity ward at St Helens hospital, right on time. Like most babies, she came screaming into the world. Soon the infant was being cradled, wrapped in a white blanket, by her mother. Isobel bent down and kissing the tiny nose swore to the child that no matter what the future held they would face it together. It was not uncommon in those days that the men folk would be asked to wait outside until all the business was finished. Therefore, it was with some trepidation that husband Aaron entered the room. He quickly and quietly hugged them both, the relief written all over his face. In a few days, they would all go home and take those few tentative steps into what would become their family life together.

Like all new mothers, Isobel often wondered if she was doing the right thing whenever Marsha was threatened with some terrible childhood illnesses. The local children's services assured her that she was doing just fine and that Marsha was developing nicely by meeting those milestones that are typical of a normal child. By ten months Marsha was beginning to attempt to crawl but pretty soon after this she started to walk. It was also safe to report that Marsha was quite the chatterbox and seemed to be able to pick up new words and phrases at a reasonable pace. Getting her to stop was what was proving to be the challenge.

Aaron and Isobel were delighted and proud that they had such a perfect child as Marsha proved to be. Isobel and Aaron ran a small grocery store just outside of the town's main thoroughfare and were very busy but they somehow managed to juggle childcare arrangements so that Marsha was well looked after. As parents, they soon realised that the good behaviour and fine manners of their daughter would reflect well on them. Marsha easily made friends and seemed such a caring person. There were the inevitable tantrums that childhood brings but thankfully these were few and far between.

As Marsha grew she was soon ready to attend school, a daunting experience for any parent let alone the child themselves. Isobel was aware that her daughter would now come under the influence of others and could only hope that Marsha's good common sense would prevail. This proved to be the case for all through primary school Marsha thrived and soaked up the knowledge given.

It was only when entering "big" school that Marsha's temperament began to break down because she was bullied, cajoled and told that she was useless almost every day by a group of older students. When Isobel became aware of what was going on at school she tried in vain to protect her daughter. However, the damage was done and there were days in which Marsha would visibly shrink a few inches and disappear to her room. It was during those periods of solitude and quiet contemplation that Marsha vowed that no-one would ever do that to her daughter and get away with it. She wanted to leave school as soon as she could and now did not care about the consequences of having little or no qualifications.

Marsha managed to get a job in the local bakery and she could be found at all hours of the day making her way home, stumbling, and covered in so much flour that she looked like a ghost. It wasn't much of a job and the money was rubbish but at least wasn't school. It was this that kept her going all week. In daydreams, she wished that somebody would come and sweep her off her feet to a new, better and more exciting life.

***

Marsha remembered her past life (and meeting the Devil) only in dreams and nightmares. She would often dream that she was cast in stone, and she would awake from these nightmares feverish and sweating. The Devil would appear to her too, swinging his tail and flexing his pointy horns, and these horrors would leave her feeling frightened and cowed for the rest of the next day and sometimes for the remainder of the week. She had no idea that these were memories of her past life lingering in her unconscious mind; she simply knew that she dreamed and she often remembered what her dreams were about when she awoke.

***

Perhaps some things in life are meant to be. Free will versus fate. Who really has the answer to that one?

In her second life, during her second time around, Marsha was walking home from work, covered lightly in flour, when she stopped into the Post Office to post a letter. As she walked towards the letterbox, she bumped into a gentleman in a long grey coat and dropped her letter. She bent down to pick it up but he beat her to it, taking the white envelope in his hand and pressing it gently into hers. Their eyes locked – freeze frame. He extended his hand.

"Please", he said. "Allow me to introduce myself. I'm Don. Don the picker-upper of letters."

Marsha laughed. She walked the few steps to the letterbox, posted the letter, then turned around and looked at Don again.

"Fancy a cup of coffee?" asked Don, summoning his courage.

"Sure, why not?"

Marsha reached up and brushed some flour off her cheek.

Marsha followed Don the short distance to Harrelson's café. Marsha ordered a cappuccino and Don ordered a flat white. They sat opposite each other at the table, sipping their coffees. For a good five minutes neither spoke, they simply sat staring at one another, mildly smitten, though each had only just made the other's acquaintance.

Something was in the air. They were two like two trains on a single track, destined to meet at some romantic junction. Marsha was only eighteen and Don twenty-three; a huge age gap at that time in their lives. She was not so world wise as he and, she thought, that this could only benefit her. It was not long before they both felt ready to commit to a more settled existence and they married. A mere ten months later Marsha gave birth to a little girl. They named her Ingrid after Marsha's Great

Grandmother. Don commented at the time Ingrid was first introduced to him, "By God she's just like you Marsha".

It therefore came as no surprise that with loving parents Ingrid not only thrived but astounded all those around her with her grasp of language and social skills. Ingrid's upbringing seemed to flash by in a blur. One minute Ingrid was a small child balancing on her mother's knee, Marsha thought when she sat watching the coals glow red in the darkened living room, and the next she is this beautiful eighteen year old with a boyfriend called Tony who seemed to have good prospects. Of course it was too early to know if anything might develop from the relationship so everybody would have to wait and see.

The parachute jump was a gift from her boyfriend. After a day of training, Ingrid booked in for the jump on Wednesday the 9th of March 2015. The day dawned fine and clear and Ingrid set out from home with a spring in her step. She had no real worries, no real cares. She was eighteen; she was full of the joys of life. She loved her parents and her boyfriend. She was about to fall from the sky.
She walked into the reception area and handed across her ticket, then made her way to the aircraft hanger where she greeted several men.
"Hello," she said. "I'm here for a solo jump. Without a static line please."
"Right you are."
One of the men handed Ingrid her parachute and showed her how to put it on. Butterflies danced in her stomach. She took a deep breath. She boarded the plane.

The plane flew high into the clear blue sky. When they reached 12,000 feet the plane levelled off. Ingrid did as her training had taught her to do and walked to the door of the plane, looking out rather than down to combat vertigo. She tucked her feet beneath the plane and launched herself out into empty space. As instructed, she allowed herself to fall for the requisite sixty seconds, before reaching for the cord of the parachute. The parachute had not been packed correctly and the chute failed to open. Ingrid fell and kept falling. She hit the ground, her neck snapped and she was killed instantly. The Devil had come to collect.

Those Left Behind

Samuel was the first to go, then little Elijah. Leaving the biblical theme behind, Kylie was next and then Karen. *Whoosh*, up they went in a blaze of white light and glory, leaving those still earthbound with mouths agape in wonder. Of those left behind, half banged their school books up and down in riot and half huddled beside the radiator, terrified that they would be chosen next. But what exactly were they so frightened of? Wasn't paradise supposed to await those who were taken up; a land of milk and honey? Shouldn't being sucked up into the heavens be exciting instead of terrifying? From the look of it, it was like being inside a tornado, with the chosen victim whirling around and around as if they were inside a gigantic washing machine. The teacher was struggling to gain control of the rioting kids. She thumped her hand on the desk and called for silence. Outside, in the Peckham street, the traffic tooted and people revved their engines as if they somehow knew what was going on inside the classroom. The kids, who were around eight years of age, continued with their anarchy, slamming the lids of their desks up and down, running senselessly around the classroom, terrified in case they were picked next, yelling out to one another. A few sat cowering in the corner, sucking their thumbs or wringing their hands; they had wet themselves from fear. The teacher had no control at all over these youngsters who most likely thought they would be next in line to be sucked up into the heavens. God only knew what was going through their minds at the time.

And those who really *did* make it to heaven - what were their thoughts? It wasn't the peaceful, serene place that many on earth touted it to be. Heaven was dark and full of storms. God was thunderous and vengeful; a grumpy old man with a beard. Who wanted to cohabit with Him? The angels had departed years before, come down to Earth in disguise or gone to hell where there was more of a party going on and a bit of a sauna to boot. Heaven's new arrivals felt disgruntled, cheated. Back on earth they'd been sold dreams of a better life, of Elysian fields - their pastor had led them to believe that once taken up they'd reside in a world of soft fluffy clouds and sweet nectar but the real truth wasn't like that at all.

They didn't have bodies now, they'd left those cumbersome entities behind – they were pure spirit; clean and neat – feeling like a heroin addict after a fix or an anorexic on a starvation high. They could be invisible at will. They hung around, looking for harps (there weren't any – more disappointment). They got so bored they nagged God incessantly until he agreed to host a heavenly mini-Olympics complete with javelin, shotput, 500m, long jump, high jump and various swimming races.

Outside the pearly gates, which were not pearly at all but run-down and rusted looking (how had *that* happened) there was a rather long queue of people all clutching tickets and waiting to get into heaven. Every hour God would pick up his megaphone and bellow out instructions in a manner strangely reminiscent of Hi-de-Hi! and announce that it was time for the worship and praise session.

Now that those who had been taken up were angels, their main duties were to serve God and to pass his messages on to people who still lived on Earth. God would whisper His message into their ear and then they would, in the wink of an eye, transport themselves to Earth in order to convey the message to its intended recipient. The messages varied and were often passed on at night when the person was dreaming. It could be a strong message that your life was in danger from another person, or it could be a more gentle hint that it was time to change job, or a whispered warning not to get on a certain aeroplane at a specific time. Some people were more receptive to these messages than others, being more highly attuned. Some people didn't want to hear. The spirits also provided food to some of the world's needy, Mother Theresa style, and helped to keep people out of danger. They would give warnings that would often take the form of premonitions. These would occur when somebody was driving too fast, standing too close to a fire, or next to a faulty windowpane that was about to shatter and injure somebody.

As spirits it was also one of their duties to release people who had been wrongfully imprisoned, for instance journalists in countries such as Egypt, Iran and Israel – political prisoners, people who had done no harm other than speak up against oppression or practice freedom of speech in a country where no such freedom was allowed. The spirits could pick locks, temporarily blind the guards, set you free in the dead of night. They also visited psychiatric hospitals where they soothed distressed souls who were being restrained, secluded or forcibly medicated. They worked wherever injustice was to be found.

God was a harsh taskmaster. Anybody who could punish Eve just for taking a bite of an apple was not to be trifled with. Why should too much knowledge mean pain in childbirth and instant obedience to a husband for ever after? At the end of each day the new recruits had to make themselves accountable to Him by giving a summary of that day's events; reporting back from the frontline. You were fully answerable for your work. The spirits were dutiful, full of praise and glory, bowing before God.

Back in the Peckham classroom the kids were still running wild. The teacher was outside crying because she hadn't been sucked up to heaven even though she'd been going to church all those years. Seeing that there was no teacher in the room, half the kids in the class ran outside and down to the nearest estate where they picked up old cigarette butts and began smoking them. Nobody missed the kids who had shot up to heaven. They'd only been a bunch of bloody goody two shoes anyhow, two of them had been Jehovah's Witnesses, and the other two were always reciting the bible, spouting God at you at every given opportunity.

The teacher called her husband to come and pick her up because she couldn't cope anymore. This was only her first month out of teacher's college and it was all a bit much. Her husband arrived and said gruffly 'Are ya right, luv?' He lit up a cigarette, and they shared it, trembling. She vomited after the second puff, mostly from the strain of the day. They left without letting anybody know, got in the car and pissed off. Chaos reigned.
The bored kids in the other classrooms looked through their school window and saw the other children coming back from the estate, smoking and cried out to their own teacher.
"Hey Miss, those kids have got old fag butts hanging from their mouths."
The teacher walked to the window to check, left her own classroom to find the other class empty and then went to tell the headmaster. The headmaster summoned one of the older and more sensible children in the class to his office and asked for an account of what had happened.

That night there was a report on the 6 o'clock news.
Today in Peckham, four children mysteriously disappear from a classroom. Eyewitnesses from the scene say they were taken up 'into the sky' without leaving any damage to the classroom roof. Chisha Lombe speaks from the scene of the incident.
Footage of a chubby kid, clutching a doughnut came onto the screen.
'They just got sucked up, innit,' he said and did the bunny fingers over the head of the kid standing next to him.
The parents, also hungry for their fifteen minutes crowded around the camera, nudging each other out of the way, vying for centre stage. One of the mothers said,

"When he didn't come home for his jerk chicken I got really worried. I didn't have a clue where he'd gone. Nobody from the school even called me."

One of the posher mothers who had recently moved to Peckham from Dulwich, her husband having lost his job in IT in the City, got on her high horse and said "My child has disappeared and nobody has a clue where she's gone. I want this thoroughly investigated. Somebody has to be held accountable."

The Minstry of Education said they would get involved, but in reality were completely ineffectual.

The following Monday two policemen came to the school. They talked to the teachers and several of the pupils. They entered the headmasters' office and had a quiet word. They left none the wiser.

An inexplicable mystery, one of the cops wrote in his notes, but didn't dare hand it in to his boss as an explanation.

An inexplicable mystery it was and an inexplicable mystery it remained, at least here on Earth. In the heavens they knew the answer, but God kept his secrets close to his chest and the new recruits worked in ways which seemed perplexing and strange.

Blood and Guts

Your own personal craniotomy. It seems too incredible to be true, the kind of thing that would happen to somebody else—a cousin or an old friend from high school with whom you lost touch years ago or that strange woman who used to live in the house next door to yours in Mount Albert when you were a child, the one whose double-hung windows came down upon her thumbs, trapping her, until she cried out and your father went across to rescue her. Phillips, you seem to recall was her name, Mrs. Phillips.

You were too young to realize then the complexity of the labyrinth you were immersed in. The complex web of family relationships that surrounded you. You had never seen your father cry. You could not comprehend public versus private. You did not understand the way in which the vast majority of people have two masks; the way in which we, as humans, present one face to the world, Eleanor Rigby–style, and have another private self that we keep well hidden, the Ace to be played at the last minute, the trump card; how much of life is a game of push- and-pull, give-and-take, one-upmanship. You still thought the world was a kind place. You hadn't learned yet that nobody respects a pushover, that the strong devour the weak and then sit gloating, munching on the bones, fresh blood dripping from one corner of the mouth. As she was for many New Zealanders, Janet Frame was the one who introduced you to the horrors of mental institutions. When her biographies were released, you witnessed firsthand the suburban schadenfreude, a Kiwi Heart of Darkness with its very own version of "The horror! The horror!" You accompanied your mother when she went to visit a friend whose husband worked with your father, and the two of them sipped tea, munched biccies and gossiped about To The Is-land, relieved that it was Janet who had suffered and not them. Mental illness was hush-hush, taboo. Most cities of any size had their own institutions; yours had Ngawatu, the remains of which still stand—the old villas and the 1920s houses where the doctors lived, the tennis court, and the bowling green. it even had its own shop where the patients could spend their "pocket money." even the most unimaginative individual could easily picture the villas being haunted by the ghosts of inmates past. The gardens are beautiful, well maintained even to this day by a caretaker who lives in a ramshackle house on the grounds. The rhododendrons bloom; the natives, kanuka and manuka, blossom; and the bulbs, jonquils, daffodils, and freesias, burst into flower.

***

The gardens are lovely, although I have no idea how many of the patients were allowed to roam freely and what restrictions were imposed upon their liberties. Doctoring, like lawyering, is not a business of black and white, but—at the risk of sounding like the recently released Mummy porn that has been flooding the market—contains many shades of grey. Lawyers deal in "legal" or "illegal," although of course there is plenty of room for shark-like maneuvering. Shrinks deal in "well" and "unwell," so there's plenty of maneuvering in that profession too. The more cynical among us would call them glorified pill dispensers. What do we do when the brain goes haywire? Behavior is analyzed and then diagnosed. Major depressive disorder, bipolar, organic brain syndrome, Asperger's, ADHD, epilepsy, anxiety, PTSD, paranoia, delusions, obsessive compulsive, schizophrenia, dissociative personality disorder, paranoid schizophrenia, psychosis. The treatment is dished up: pills, the depot (an injection, typically administered fortnightly), ECT, seclusion, restraint, insulin therapy, IPC. I speak in defense of the patients—somebody has to. in any setting other than a psychiatric institution, a lot of what takes place would constitute human rights abuse. Oh, I know, I know, there are the posters on the wall—Your Rights—but it's all fairly tokenistic. Toothless. Prison might be better. At least a prison sentence has an end date, and there's always the chance that they'll release you early on good behavior. or if you can stump up bail. or get a good lawyer. But the vast majority of psychiatric patients will have access to neither. You can be kept in a psychiatric institution, or Mental health Unit, indefinitely. Most of the lawyers who represent mental health patients would like to be sitting behind a swanky wooden desk, surrounded by leather-bound tomes and piles and piles of files, and pulling in six-figure sums rather than scraping the bottom of the legal aid barrel.

***

You didn't know when you were young about the Diagnostic and Statistical Manual of Mental Disorders (DsM), about ECT or insulin therapy or Monsanto. You knew nothing about Risperidone, lamotrigine, Quetiapine, Dilantin, or about the forced drugging of psychiatric patients in order to turn them into zombies who are more easily controlled (even though you had always been fond of horror stories). Death by doctoring. The three conditions for being sectioned remain the same: danger to self, danger to others, or inability to care for self. The brain is high-priced real estate— the Tokyo of the body. Private psychiatrists are represented in New Yorker cartoons, the shrinks modeling themselves on Freud, complete with couch and many a fleeing Dora. The public system is, of course, a good deal more brutal. Like the mental health lawyers who resent their colleagues who are employed in the private sector, the shrinks would undoubtedly prefer to be raking in the cash running their own Sopranos-style private practices and catering to the wealthy rather than dealing with those on benefits. Perhaps it is a grotesque generalization, but the public sector has always been more scrooge than Santa.

I recently had a craniotomy to remove a brain tumor— oligodendroglioma, grade 2, in case your granny wants to know. I was operated on at Christchurch public hospital. I had been keeping myself fit. The evening before the operation, i ate a hearty meal of steak and spuds in order to make it through in one piece. I woke up in Ward 28: Neurology. Felt fine. Was seen by the neurosurgeon, the neurosurgical registrar, and two or three nurses. Three days later, the sutures were pulled from my head and I was discharged, left to find my own way back to Ranui house. I was driven back to my parents' home for the night. Following a nightmare, I sleepwalked into my parents' room and freaked them out, and they arranged to have me put in the local Mental Health Unit. I attempted to abscond and was locked in seclusion, solitary confinement, a psychiatric version of "The hole." The lights were switched on and off all night; I spent the entire time vomiting. They moved me around from room to room (or should I say "cell to cell"?) in order to increase my sense of disorientation. The first room had nothing to see outside the window except concrete. It was a form of dungeon. A stitch- proof gown was put across the air vent to stop the draft. I could smell the murder in the walls. The second room I was moved to had a plant outside the window, so at least I had some sense of where "outside" was. I wondered if the water was poisoned. The nurses entered with drugs, which I ingested after some deliberation. They moved me to another room. The doctor came in with more drugs, which I took. What else could I do? This is how they train you to become medication compliant. The nurses seemed more interested in checking their Facebook messages and gossiping about their latest boyfriend dramas than they did in "tending" to the patients. All right boys, out the back, out the back was what they said before hauling me into seclusion. I coped by detaching myself, pretending it was a movie, something that was happening to somebody else. I wouldn't go through brain surgery again —it's ever so traumatic to have somebody else fossicking around in your frontal lobes and cingulate gyrus, especially if the aftercare provided is as horrendous as that which I received. Luckily for me, I had support workers arranged to help care for me in my own home, and so, with the help of a lawyer, I was discharged fairly quickly, bag of medication in hand. When I was diagnosed, I was given ten years to live. Now I've got six years to go. Gliomas "almost inevitably recur" and "are almost invariably fatal." The surgeon got most—but not all—of it due to infiltration, the tendrils that have invaded my brain. Time to check off a few items on the bucket list. Time to enjoy myself. I never would have parachuted before the cancer. What's the worst that can happen, I asked myself on the way up in the plane, the chute doesn't open and you die an instantaneous death rather than a prolonged and lingering one? Next up, paragliding…

Castle

Jack Davidson could fly only in his dreams.   In real life it was another story. In real life the opposite was true. Jack was wheelchair bound, his muscles weakened by muscular dystrophy, dependent on his Mum to feed him, to wash him and, most humiliating of all, to take him to the toilet. In real life Jack Davidson was a target, easy meat, prey for bully boys. He had friends too though, a small gang who gathered protectively around him, drawn by his personality. You had to have something going for you, didn't you? It's not as if he was eye candy or anything. Jack hated how weak he was. What he really wanted was strength, power, the ability to lift two hundred kilogram weights, when in reality he was struggling to lift a glass of water. He also resented the fact that he could no longer hug his Mum. When his step-brother visited he would throw his arms around Jack's Mum and Jack would be green with envy and go to his room and cry in secret. He hated for people to see him crying; that would be an admission that the illness was getting him down, affecting him deep inside. Above all else Jack Davidson wanted to be strong, a champion, a hero, able to help others when in reality he couldn't even help himself.

Jack Davidson also had a secret. A secret that kept him going, that got him through his bad days, his troubled times, his darkest hours. It was a magnificent, marvellous secret, but terrible and dangerous too. Jack had discovered a portal to other dimensions. The first time that it happened he hadn't quite believed what was occurring, what was taking place. Still, there was no mistaking what had transpired. He had been sucked right through the chessboard and into a real life version of his imagination.

Jack had no idea what the person left behind sitting at the chessboard (his Dad) was thinking. They would be mystified, surely, that was only natural. To have somebody vanish just like that, at the drop of a hat, to have a person, a *human body* disappear into thin air, how could that not create a sense of bewilderment?

He'd been thinking about elves at the time he was transported (childish, he knew, but hey, a guy can't always control his thoughts) and suddenly he found himself in some sort of Elf Land, with irritatingly happy-go-lucky little creatures dancing around him, holding hands. They seemed harmless enough at first, but then when he looked closer he noticed that some of them had knives. Fear and anger propelled him out of his wheelchair. He grabbed the nearest elf by the wrist and twisted, then karate chopped him in the elbow. The elf squealed and dropped the knife. The other elves fled in terror, fearful of meeting the same fate. Jack was delighted. He could do it! He had strength. To him it seemed marvellous, magical, a miracle. Jack looked around at the world he was in. It was outlandish but eerie as if he was on another planet; green skies and a red moon. The trees looked as if they were made of static, like a bad TV broadcast. Now that the elves had vanished there was nobody else in sight and Jack was completely alone. He decided to explore the world a little more. There was a scungy-looking river running down to his right. A pink unicorn with a golden horn appeared and he followed it along until he reached the coast. The unicorn bent down and took a drink from the river and the water became golden. Jack followed suit. He felt himself expand, enlarge. He flexed his arm and his muscles bulged. He had grown three feet and his view extended for miles around - he could see a neighbouring village in the distance. He felt that he could gaze into the universe. Now that the elves were gone it was a pleasant enough world, but it was tea time and he was hungry. He needed to find a way back, back to his Mum and the home cooked meal that would be waiting on the kitchen table. The unicorn dived into the river, swam down underneath the surface and disappeared. Jack followed it, holding his breath and diving under till he found where the unicorn had gone; into an underwater passageway, a stone cavern that lead him back to the room he had left from, the room with the chessboard.

Where the hell have you been?' his father asked, when he re-appeared on the side of the board. "You vanished."

Jack fobbed him off.

"Just went to the loo while you weren't looking. Mum met me in the corridor and helped me."

His father looked skeptical but said nothing. Jack checked the clock. Only five minutes had past, long enough for a quick loo break.

He wheeled his chair through into the kitchen where his Mum took a plate of cottage pie from the microwave and set it on the table.

'There's your dinner anyway.'

'Thanks very much.'

Jack was starving after his adventure. He hoed into the cottage pie, smothering it with tomato sauce. After dinner he went straight to bed, exhausted from the day's exciting findings.

***

Jack had experienced a particularly trying day at school. The bully boys didn't usually get physical – mostly their abuse took the form of verbal taunts and jeers. *Jack can't walk, Jack can't walk.* However, on this day which weather-wise was a grey and miserable one, as if external weather matched internal mood, two of the three bullies had bonded together and conspired to tip over Jack's wheelchair. It was malicious behaviour and far from a harmless prank; Jack put out his hands to break his fall and fractured the bone in the little finger of his right hand. He cried out in pain and the bullies danced around him in circles chanting *Jack's a cry baby, Jack's a cry baby.* Everything about the incident was awful. His protectors, his little gang of friends were nowhere in the vicinity. He was alone, horribly, utterly alone, sprawled on the ground in an undignified fashion. It was, somewhat predictably, a teacher who saved him. Good old Mrs McLary, watching the entire scenario unfold from her classroom window came rushing to his aid, righting his wheelchair and helping him back up into it. She patted his shoulder in what Jack assumed was supposed to be a reassuring fashion. It only made him feel worse, patronised. She told him he could stay in the sickbay for the afternoon. Jack was bored silly in the sick bay but he found a nurse who, discovering a chessboard in the games cupboard in the library, agreed to play the game with him. Jack had thought that the act of vanishing to another dimension when castling might have been a one-off but, no, it happened again. He castled when playing against the nurse and once again was sucked, rushing through the chessboard and into another time. He was in the school playground, on the basketball court, up and out of his wheelchair. He looked down at his clothes; he was clad in a long maroon robe with gold tassels and held a wand in his hand. Magic! He felt in his left hand pocket. There was a piece of chalk in there; he bent down and drew a circle on the ground so that he would be safe when he cast his spells. He looked out across the playground – here came the bullies now. One was smacking a fist into an open palm, the other was picking his nose. Jack felt the old terror clench in his gut, then he drew a deep breath, raised himself up to full height and pointed his wand at the bullies, muttering 'Cravius blind mouses'...

It worked! Jack could hardly believe his eyes but now, heading his way were not three bullies, but three blind mice. He could step on them if he wanted. He could put them in a sack and drown them. He could destroy them, easily and on a whim. Jack picked up the mice by their tails, walked with them down to the stream that ran along the back of the school and drowned them, one by one. He then made his way to the sick bay, where a chess board was set up, moved his queen to take a rook and found himself back in his prior time.

***

The next day at school assembly there was an announcement. Three boys had drowned off the coast, near Velware Rock. Three names were read out – they were the three boys who had taunted Jack the previous day. Jack felt a pang of guilt travel through him. Had he really been responsible for their deaths? By turning them into mice and drowning them, had he somehow magically, crazily, brought about their destruction in real life? If so, Jack wasn't sure how he felt about being a murderer. They had bullied him, but he had killed them. Surely that was the worse sin and God, if He was looking down from the heavens, would not look favourably upon a killer, even if there had been mitigating circumstances.

***

The next time Jack castled he was thinking of the family cat. He found himself in cat land, surrounded by snooty, independent cats. The nearest one was snacking on a mouse.

"How come you cats get to prance and pounce all day when I'm stuck in a wheelchair", asked Jack.

"In this land you are no longer a cripple. Come on, get up out of that wheelchair and walk."

One of the cats let out a soft meow. Jack put one hand either side of his wheelchair and pushed himself up to his feet. He put his left foot forward in front of his right, then his right foot forward in front of his left. Step by step, that was the way. He looked down at his shoes – he was walking! It was a miracle. It would have been a spectacle had there been spectators, but no humans were present, just the cats, who seemed remarkably under impressed, just going about their business. One was licking its front paws clean, another was sharpening its claws upon a tree. Jack wished there was a witness, somebody there to take a photograph or make a drawing of this, his most marvellous moment in years, but nobody was around. He lay down on the ground, closed his eyes and wished himself back home.

***

The scariest castling of all occurred when Jack was thinking of the dangers posed to him by the white tail spider that was crawling across the chessboard when he swapped his rook and his king. He found himself transported to the centre of a vast, dark cave whose walls were spun with sticky webs. At one end of the cave, blocking the exit, sat an enormous Shelob-style spider possessed of great hairy legs as thick as punga logs, glistening red eyes and enormous fangs that hung down low. Jack was terrified. This spider could eat him alive. He backed away, tentatively, slowly, to the opposite end of the cave, sat down on the ground and took a swig from his thermos. He'd been clutching it when he castled, thank God - it was thirsty work hovering just metres from a forbidding spider, and he took a long swig from the thermos. He felt in his left hand pocket. It was there, the wand. Thanking God for large mercies, Jack withdrew the wand and waved it in the direction of the spider. Immediately, it diminished in size, shrinking smaller and smaller until it was no larger than the size of fifty pence. Jack could have done anything. He could have stomped on the spider. He could have enticed it onto a piece of paper and carried it to a different place. He could have

51

trimmed one of its legs. Jack didn't do any of these things. Instead he walked past the spider and out through the exit, via the path that the spider had previously blocked. The cave's exit became the entrance to his home and he walked in through the front door to find his mother taking a tray of freshly baked meringues from the oven.

***

Jack's Dad, Gullivar, who was an astronomer, had given Jack a copy of *Dark Energy For Dummies* for Christmas in an effort to get his son interested in his own field. After dinner on Monday night, Jack sat down to play his Dad at chess. *Dark Energy For Dummies* sat beside the chessboard. Jack waited until his Dad had his knights out and into the game, then cleared the spaces between his rook and his king and castled. *Woosh.* There was a great sucking of air, as if Jack was being engulfed into a vacuum. He found himself on a planet of pure gravity. An invisible planet, an unseen realm, at a constant temperature, hot but not so warm that Jack couldn't stand it. A world comprised of dark matter. To the left of him sat a darkly glowing orb. Jack looked into it and saw a future version of himself, lying bedridden at home. He shuddered and wiped the orb with his hankie. This time it showed him a happier vision; his parents together on a Pacific Cruise. Jack put out his right hand, and picked up the orb and was immediately transported back to his house, still clutching the orb in his hand.

***

Back at home Jack began feeling the effects of having been in a world comprised of dark matter. He felt empty, drained. The gamma rays produced by the annihilation of dark matter had proved harmful and damaging to his body. He slept badly that night, tossing and turning and haunted by nightmares, terrible dreams that stuck with him far into the next day. When he finally did get out of bed he wondered if the bad dreams might not be in some way connected to the orb and he took it through into his father's study and resolved never to look into it again, so frightened was he of the vision of his dying self he had seen therein.

***

The land of robots was the most helpful place that Jack visited. All sorts of robots were there for the taking. There were robots dancing in synchronicity, robots doing the cleaning, robots making other robots, and lazy robots just sitting around doing nothing.

A short, fat man with a loudhailer seemed to be in charge. Jack approached cautiously.

"Err, hello," he said. "I wanted to enquire about the cost of these 'bots.'"

Jack patted his wallet, trying to give the impression that he was flush with cash. His mother gave him pocket money and he had been saving it up for several years.

"Selling cheap. The cleaners are $50, the dancers are $60. The lazy robots are for free. "

Jack took one of the cleaning robots, intending to take it home for his Mum. The robot was made out of titanium and had a microcontroller for a brain.

"Say", he said, sidling a little closer. "You haven't got anything that could help out with….with a *person*, have you?"

"*A person?* What do you mean help out with a *person?*"

"Well it's like this. I know I can walk in this world, but back in my world I have muscular dystrophy and am confined to a wheelchair. It's a real pain and my Mum has to do absolutely *everything* for me. Have you got a 'bot that could help her take care of me?"

"Let's see now. You want the HHH – the Handy Home Helper. Can feed you, wipe ya bum and give you a shower. Not all at the same time mind you."

Jack's ears perked up.

"How much?"

"$99.95 A bargain at twice the price."

Jack wondered about the quality of the goods he was buying, given the cheapness, but he took them anyway.

"Say, got anything that could help with teleportation?"

"You betcha."

A small red droid exchanged hands. Jack held it out in front of him and was teleported back home to his Mum, clutching a robot under either arm.

***

Back at home, he delivered the robots to his mother and explained what they did. She was thrilled at the new home help and what it signified – namely, a significant diminishment of her workload. It freed her up to spend more time with Jack, talking with him, reading to him and holding his hand.

***

The most exciting land that Jack visited was the land of fantasy. This was a place where unicorns, griffins, green panda and lightening leopards roamed free. Ruling this land was a lady called Lavender who wore a gingham purple and white dress and carried a black wand that sparkled in the sunlight. She offered to give Jack a tour of the land which was the most beautiful place he had ever seen, blessed with swiftly flowing rivers, snow capped mountains and waterfalls which tumbled down from a great height. Jack was in awe of the landscape and looked around him, mouth agape, taking in its splendour. Lavender took Jack by the hand and together they went wading into one of the nearby streams. The water splashed playfully around their ankles. This was one land that Jack did not want to leave. As evening drew in the giants came out to play. They had been hiding in caves, fearful of the sunlight but as soon as the sun began to go down they came forth. They leapt over ravines and rivers, took it all in gigantic stride and Jack began to feel himself swell and expand too, growing larger and larger, as if he had drunk of some magical elixir like Alice in Wonderland. Now he was *Superjack*, stronger than strong, capable of lifting boulders and throwing whole cars out of his way, a cripple transformed. A World Warrior, travelling through space and time, doing magic, doing good. One of the giants invited Jack back to his lair for a cup of tea, stirring in three teaspoons of sugar. Feeling a little guilty, Jack pocketed the spoon as a souvenir to take back and show his Mum.

At eight pm a bell rang, a bell that sounded terrible to Jack's ears as he knew it would summon him back to the real world. Sure enough, soon after the bell had rung, the glorious vision that was the land of fantasy began to pale and fade and Jack found himself back in the real world, in his own small home sitting opposite his mother at the kitchen table. Jack found himself clutching what, in the land of the giants had been a teaspoon but which was, in this world, the size of a spade. He handed it to her mother and told her she could use it for her gardening. Jack's mother was a saint. Because of his disease she had to do everything for her son although she was aided now by robots. Of course, she could have put him into a care home but she was too kind-hearted to do this. The thought of giving up her son was more than she could bear and so she took upon herself the many tasks associated with being a sole caregiver. She lifted Jack on and off the toilet and wiped his bottom for him. She chopped his meals into bite sized pieces and fed him with a fork. She bathed him every night in soapy water and cleaned his teeth for him. She tried hard not to show the burden that she felt. If the Lord had chosen to try her in this way then so be it, she was not one to complain or make a fuss.

The following day Jack's mother was gardening with her new shovel in the vegetable patch down at the end of the garden, when it broke free from her hands and started doing the digging for her all on its own. She stood back, put her hands on her hips and exclaimed "Well, I never, a self-digging shovel. Where on earth did you get this from Jack!" The shovel dug on, oblivious to criticism or praise until it had turned the entire vegetable garden and dug a series of neat furrows all ready for planting.

***

The most intellectually challenging world that Jack visited was chess land. It was when he was playing chess with his Dad that he castled into chess land and then castled again from the giant chess board in chess land to his deepest darkest nightmares. They were so bad that when he

54

went home he had bad dreams for a week. The nightmares were of his muscular dystrophy getting worse and him dying very, very slowly.

The most spellbinding adventure was when he went to the land of water. Under the water were all manner of different and interesting creatures that lived under the sea.   He also realized, when he castled to this dimension, that he could breathe underwater and talk to the various ocean creatures that he met. After an hour in the water conversing with dolphins and whales and tropical fish, it was time to go home; back to the death bed.

Only Jack's Dad knew that he could travel to other dimensions and Jack was glad that he had someone to talk about it too.

"Hey Dad, I've been travelling", he said to his father, one day after dinner.

"*Travelling?* What do you mean *travelling?*"

"Venturing far and wide."

"Who with?"

"Just on my own. Via a chess board."

"Via a chess board. Whadda ya mean 'via a chess board'. You can't travel using a chess board.'"

"Yes you can. When I castle I go to other dimensions. It's fantastic. I would offer to take you with me, but I think these are trips I have to make solo."

***

The most treacherous land was the land of danger. It had snakes, bears, dragons, and Venus fly traps that ate humans. While Jack was walking along the dirt path a Venus fly trap tried to grab him but he turned it into a harmless rose petal and loads of skulls and bones full out. *Phew* he thought *that was a close one.* He decided to go home before any more bad things happened to him. Back to the death bed he thought grimly. He tapped one of the bones that had fallen out of the Venus fly trap against his thigh, and found himself back at home in his wheelchair.

***

The most joyful world was the land of good luck where there were always happy and merry people. There was happiness and laughter in the air you could just sense it. Here the people were all happy no matter what they had. Unlike the land of bad luck it was a land of joy and laughter.

***

The complete opposite of the land of good luck was the land of bad luck. It was a monstrous place with loads of horrific and terrifying things happening. There were tons of graveyards and dead people and everyone was sad and miserable. There were also heaps of people in poverty with no food and it was raining all the time. Jack didn't stay there that long because he couldn't bear to see such misery. There were many skeletons in this world; the skeletons of people who had died in nasty ways and their spirits hadn't crossed over to the other side properly. They were haunted people, hungry people and people who had died in distress. Jack didn't like to see so much suffering so he tried to make them happy, but they were tortured souls. He tried to cheer them up by doing magic tricks and clowning around. The weather in the land of bad luck was always thunderstorms and rain. Jack did a dance which was the opposite of a rain dance and the sun came out and shone, albeit a little weakly. The skeletons rose up and joined in the dance too and Jack was glad to have brought a little joy to this dull and bleak place.

Back in the real world, Jack's muscular dystrophy progressed. He grew weaker and more distressed with each passing day. As he lay on his death bed, his father sat down to play a game of chess with him.

'Go on then son, choose. Which dimension will you pick as your final destination?'

Jack closed his eyes and thought of his idea of heaven. There would be fields of beautiful flowers, a sun that always shone and idyllic beaches. He castled and then he was there, transported to his imagined destination, his own heaven. Jack Davidson had earned his passport to paradise.

Catfishing

I set the honey trap on a Sunday, the official day of rest. Hi my name is Nadia and I'm a support worker which means I help a lady who has had a brain tumour removed function in her day to day life. Three months ago I moved in with the man who was supposed to be the love of my life. We met on an online dating site – NZDating.com. When I first met him he threw his arms around me and gave me a great big bear hug and I'd never felt so safe and warm. Gordon his name was – Gordie for short. Being in his arms felt like coming home.

I haven't had the greatest life. My mum had ten kids on a benefit so most of us became foster children. I wouldn't know what family I would be with from one month to the next. I did my best to behave so some family would adopt me permanently, but nobody ever did.

Then fate or God or nature threw me yet another horrible curve ball. I care for my son who has muscular dystrophy. I don't mean to say that my son was the curve ball because I love him dearly, but the MD was. When the doctor broke that news to me I went home and cried for three hours straight then cracked open a bottle of vodka and proceeded to get rip roaring drunk on my own. Jack's Dad upped and left when he heard the news, didn't want to stick around to help look after a disabled kid. Poor Jack – condemned to a life with faulty muscles. He has to have major surgery this month – they're putting metal rods in his spine and clipping his tendons.

But I digress – just filling you in on some of the background of my life. This story is about the honeytrap and how I set it.

I suspected my man of cheating on me. There had been numerous trips to a nearby town – 'work trips' that smelt of an affair. I'd found a half used lipstick that didn't belong to me under the passenger seat of his ute. Another woman's belongings. I made my way to my friend's house and logged on to NZ Dating as her. I found his profile easily enough; it didn't look like he'd changed it since I'd met him on there. He'd lied about his age. As myself, I had a date set up with him for that Tuesday; he'd agreed to take me ice skating. Pretending to be my friend, I started chatting him up, asking him about his life and his work. Oblivious to the fact that it was me, he played along, which made me feel sick to my stomach, just thinking that this alone is cheating on his behalf. I wanted to confront him then and there but knew that I needed for him to meet me in person in order to give him more rope to hang himself with, just to see if he would follow through with meeting another woman. Just as I was thinking that a message came through from him. And so the deceit began. The messages read as follows.

Gordon: 'When are you free would love to meet up?'

Nadia (posing as Cynthia): 'How about Tuesday?'

Gordon: 'Sorry I'm busy Tuesday. Spending time with my son. What about Wednesday evening?'

Cynthia: Sure that's fine. It's good that you're spending time with your son, what a nice dad.'

Gordon: Well, I try.

Cynthia: Where shall I meet you? At a bar or restaurant?

Gordon: Sure a bar sounds good. Do you know Moonlighters?

Cynthia: I sure do. See you there at around 8.

Gordon: Okay looking forward to meeting you Sweetie.

On Wednesday evening I set off to meet my cheating boyfriend. Just to rub it in his face a bit more I made sure I looked damned good that day too. He was waiting for me, or waiting for Cynthia, on a bar stool near the front of Moonlighters, looking rather pleased with himself until he saw me.

"Oh hi Nadia, what are you doing here?"

"More to the question what are *you* doing here?" I replied.

He scrambled for words and tried to blurt out 'I'm meeting a colleague here.'

"Don't you mean Cynthia" I snarkily replied.

"Who's Cynthia?"

"The girl you've been chatting up on NZDating you scum of the earth. And you even had the gall to say you were spending time with your son." His silence spoke volumes. I walked from the bar, thinking that if I didn't I might rip his skin from his bones. He was so gutless he didn't even have the balls to chase after me, he just let me walk away. A word for the wise – stay off dating sites in fact, maybe stay off men altogether.

Old Hat

Originally the hat had belonged to old Mrs Pembleton, a widow who lived at 3 Marshes Lane. It had been discovered at the back of the wardrobe where it had sat gathering dust and the wings of old moths. It wasn't much to look at and nothing about it spoke of special powers. It was black velvet on the outside and purple velvet on the inside. It was plush in places but worn in others, like a well-loved teddy bear. Sophie's parents had bought the house off Mrs Pembleton shortly after Mr Pembleton had died. Sophie had stumbled across the hat on a Sunday when she had been bored and exploring the nooks and crannies of the home.

Sophie tried on the hat in front of the hallway mirror. She turned to the left and then to the right, vainly admiring her own reflection. Sophie was nine and she was being bullied at school by a gang of older girls. She spoke aloud.

"Oh I wish I didn't have to go to school tomorrow", she said.

The tip of the hat twitched a little to the right.

That evening Sophie complained to her mother that she wasn't feeling well. Her mother took her temperature and found it be 102 degrees Celsius.

"Gosh," said her mother. "You've got a raging fever. Best you stay home tomorrow."

It was the result Sophie had been hoping and praying for. Later, after she had changed into her pyjamas, she noticed that her throat was extraordinarily sore and in the morning her glands were swollen into large lumps on both sides of her neck. She ran to find her mother and showed her the offending swellings.

"Oh no", said her mother. "It looks like you've got a nasty case of the mumps. You must've caught it off somebody at school. We'd better get you to the doctor."

The doctor confirmed the diagnosis and prescribed bedrest, fluids and pain relief. Sophie went home and took to her bed. After ten days the mumps had subsided and Sophie was able to move freely about the house again.

Nobody thought too much about more about the hat until it was put into a garage sale. It was purchased by Clive Stevenson, a lawyer in the City who wanted it for a fancy dress party. He was going dressed as a wizard and thought that the hat suited the part. He had a matching purple wand with a lightning bolt on it to go with the outfit. The fancy dress party had been organized by his law firm as a special end of year event celebrating their financial success throughout the year. Clive was pretty fed up and jaded with the corporate world. It had lost its allure. The money no longer compensation for the stress. The work/life balance didn't balance anymore. He had been secretly wishing for a life free from the rat race. He wanted time and space to pursue his passion for painting and sculpture. He was into post-modernist styles and admired the work of Tracey Emin, Damien Hirst and Gabriel Orozco. He didn't fancy that he could make great strides in the art world because he thought he was starting too late but he thought he might make some small contribution.

A month after the fancy dress party he was taking the tube home from work during what had been a particularly stressful week when he became suddenly overwhelmed by the maps, the flashing lights and the loudspeaker announcements. For two hours he tried and failed to board the correct train that would take him to his required destination, an activity he had successfully performed for over ten years. It was beyond frustrating. Unsure of how to proceed, he purchased a bottle of water and sat down upon the tube station floor, his briefcase on the floor beside him. Somebody approached to check if he was okay, then called him an ambulance.

Mr Stevenson was taken to St Guy and Thomas' and the Maudsley psychiatric hospital was called. He was initially told he had a bad case of burnout and told to take time off work to rest and recuperate. His employer granted him leave, but when he tried and failed to use the London underground during his time off, further investigations were deemed necessary. He was interviewed by Dr Brandon who listened carefully to his account of the symptoms, then ordered an MRI. A lesion was found on his brain and he was told that this was a low grade of brain tumour. Surgery was recommended. Clive went home and googled low grade glioma and came up with an article by Anders Whiterson. He contacted the author of the article who was a member of the Royal College of Neurosurgeons. The author put himself forward as a potential surgeon to do the craniotomy. After investigating his background, Clive took him up on the offer. He applied to his law firm for income protection insurance payments on the grounds of sickness and his claim was accepted.

The craniotomy was performed at the National Hospital for Neurology and Neurosurgery in Queen's Square, London. The operation was successful and an oligodendroglioma the size of three walnuts was removed from his brain. He woke up in the neurology ward. They checked that he could walk and talk, asked him to touch his finger to his nose and he was discharged two days after the operation had taken place. Clive thought it was all a bit slap-dash but what could he do?

After a week at home recovering from the surgery, Clive took the opportunity to throw himself into his artwork. He took himself to a store selling art supplies, purchased the requisite items and began to sculpt and paint. The NHS supplied him with support workers who helped him with day to day tasks and sometimes, when he asked them, with his art. After eighteen months, when he had completed a selection of mixed media pieces, he approached a number of the smaller galleries and asked them if they would hold an exhibition. He got three small nibbles and one bite. The bite was from a gallery in Peckham – Isaac's Space. They said he could hold his exhibition in the space for 50% of the profits. Knowing that this was the going rate, Clive took them up on the offer.

The exhibition was a moderate success and over half the pictures and two out of six sculptures sold. One sculpture was of an angel falling to earth; the other was of a bear with a salmon. It was more success than he had expected and he knew he had done well for a first timer recovering from a craniotomy. This inspired him to continue to follow his passion.

The hat was displayed in the exhibition and was purchased by Jacqueline Mills. Jacquie was a housewife who was married to a used car salesman. She was dissatisfied with her life and often dreamed of a better one which included moving to a better home. She had come to the gallery looking for a picture to hang on the wall at home and had fallen in love with the hat. She purchased it for $150 and took it home with her. That evening she was looking through the Property Press when she saw her dream home. It was located in the posh part of town, on the heights, and was going for half a million dollars. Cheap, suspiciously cheap, Jacquie should have thought, but she was too excited by the find to think that far.

She went to view the house the next day. It was on poles at the front and was on a fairly steep section. The real estate agent showed her around. It was a fresh modern home and she fell in love with the place. That night she talked with her husband about selling their old house and upgrading. Jacquie could usually talk her husband around to her way of thinking and on this occasion she was successful in her bid for a new home.

The requisite papers were signed and they shifted into their contemporary home two months later. The following night, at around midnight, there was an earthquake measuring 7.5 on the Richter scale. The piles of the house shifted and the entire house became uneven and unable to be lived in. For the first time, the hat was blamed. Jacquie thought the hat was unlucky and took it to the local Salvation Army shop to get rid of it.

The hat sat in the Salvation Army shop for a week before being picked up by Earnest Dingleman who worked in the shop. He took it back to the rest home where he was also employed part-time. He walked into the dining hall that evening carrying the hat in his hands.
"Hey", a voice cried out from the other side of the hall. "That's my hat!" Earnest looked over in the direction where the voice was coming from.
It was Mrs Pembleton, who had been in the rest home for only six weeks, a new recruit. Earnest took the hat over to where she sat. Mrs Pembleton took the hat from him gratefully, lovingly, and placed it on her head. It looked like it belonged there, as if it had finally come home.

Now that it had been reunited with its owner, the hat stopped playing the naughty genie. Mrs Pembleton, who had been been playing up in the rest home, not going to bed on time and waking at all hours of the night and early morning and waking other people up with her walking cane, also calmed down eased more gracefully into life in the retirement home. She had also been refused to eat properly, but once she had been reunited with the hat, all that changed and she began to consume proper meals. The hat settled down and began to grant people in the rest home their wishes without any dark twist. It listened into conversations and picked up on people's dreams and hopes and did its best to make them come true. When Ms Clivedale wished for her son to come and visit her, the hat did its best to arrange this. Ms Clivedale's son was a lawyer and she felt that he had no time for her, but when he visited just after Xmas some of her fears were erased. When Mr Bantam prayed for his son to return home safely from Afghanistan, the hat took care of it. Mrs Hilary dreamed of a third grandchild and her daughter gave birth to little Ingrid, a healthy baby girl, that June.

Mrs Pembleton died the following January and the hat was buried with her. If you walk in past the gates of the cemetery you can see where they are buried, just there on the right, next to Mr Pembleton, with their names engraved on the headstone.

Boris v Shelob

Danny and I were in our office in the S.O.C.A. – the Serious Organised Crime Agency – when Gillian came through with the two prototypes. She held them out on the palm of her hand. They were identical except for the removable stickers upon their thoraxes. Boris, who had been manufactured by the Russians, had a sticker with a red, white and blue stripe running along it. Shelob, a German prototype, had a yellow, black and red stripe across hers. Shelob was battery-powered. A couple of years ago, somewhere around 2018, the Russians had figured out how to power radio telephones and field equipment with vodka, so Boris had a tiny vodka-pack stashed under his thorax which he used for fuel.

The two spiders were to be pitted against one another in a dummy run that Danny liked to joke had parallels with Amundsen and Scott's race to the North Pole. On the surface they seemed like ordinary spiders; eight legs, bodies divided into two segments – the thorax and the abdomen. Look closer and you would see that both insects were robots in disguise; they were masterpieces of modern design – objects of beauty. Both were installed with two-way radios to allow messages to be sent and received. Both were semi-autonomous: half the intelligence was in the beast and half was in the base station. Dedicated electronic controllers were kept at the crime unit. Encrypted communications, to prevent interference, were sent back and forth between spider and controller. The arachnids were fitted with audio and visual equipment that enabled them to provide live feedback to the Police Commissioner's office. They were also given a sense of smell that enabled them to sniff out ganja. The audio feedback was used to direct the servomotor in relation to what it was controlling – the movement of the legs and leg joints, the pitch, roll and yaw of the body. As the name would suggest, the controller knows what has to happen, 'move left leg forward', 'twitch right leg twice', etc. It gets feedback about leg position, and therefore keeps the spider's body parts under control. The software allows various parameters to be monitored – crawl speed, eye movement, leg synchronicity, the position of the body in relation to the legs. The spiders' hardware utilizes nano-technology – the motors that control its motion, the nano-eyes so that its controller can sense what is around it.

Over the last decade great progress had been made in the field of biomimicry – the copying of nature's structure and skills to solve technical conundrums. In contrast to the past, when humans tried to subjugate nature, we were now trying to learn from the animals. Millions of years of natural selection can't be wrong. Take the Fresco bird, for instance: a prime example of art meets engineering. Modelled on the herring gull, the team at Fresco had designed a robotic bird with superior powers of flight. Inspired by this, teams in Russia and Frankfurt had developed spiders that could be sent in to crime scenes. The prototypes had been created two years afterwards by a team in Frankfurt and shipped out to New Zealand in moderate numbers to be tested in a relatively confined environment – the Antipodes, such as was done with EFTPOS. Both robots closely mimicked the movements of real spiders; hydraulically-operated limbs provide great stability in uneven terrain. In contrast with the gecko that had been manufactured by the same Frankfurt team which could scale any elevation, the spider could walk horizontally, but not vertically.

Word had reached the Crime Unit that pot was being grown in Milkwood Road by a gang of bikers known as Hell's Spawn, so naturally Danny wanted to send the spiders in to investigate.

It was the arachnid's first run and we didn't give them anything terribly spectacular to tackle. We didn't set them to spy on a cocaine ring, or anything particularly important. We could've sent them in to bust a serious crime; Class A drugs, people-smuggling, human trafficking, major gun crime, fraud, computer crime or money laundering, but for this, their dummy run, we just gave them the task of sniffing out who in Milkwood Road was growing ganja. Whichever spider returned the correct information regarding the location of the pot, thus enabling the drug ring to be busted, would be selected as the S.O.C.A.'s spider of choice.

After inspection and testing, Danny declared both Shelob and Boris fit to release on assignment. Boris performed well during testing, but Shelob was behaving in a curious manner. Was I the only one who had noticed the strangely spasming eighth leg? The twitching left eye? Perhaps the poor thing was having seizures. They'd accidentally programmed it to have a touch of epilepsy. Mind you, who could feel sorry for a robot – a created entity that could not feel, at least not yet, not in this decade and probably not in my generation. Danny was our boss, so if he said it was ready for release, then Gillian and I had no choice but to go along with it. I kept my doubts about Shelob to myself. I didn't want Danny to think that I was getting too big for my boots in case he took out his managerial scalpel and cut me down to size.

Gillian said that we should bet on which of the spiders would correctly locate the house with the ganja and that he was going to place his odds on Shelob because he didn't believe that a vodka-powered robot could go the distance. Danny declared that the smart money was on Boris, and that this opinion was based on Shelob's twitching leg which he thought would cause problems during the covert operation, either by reducing his crawl speed or else by blowing his cover.

The two spiders were dropped off at the end of Milkwood Road. Shelob took off in the wrong direction, scuttling down Shakespeare Road by accident. She was corrected via audio instructions radioed in from HQ by Danny. Shelob's audio feedback came through before the visuals. It was broadcast back to HQ in real time and differed significantly from what Danny and team had been anticipating. Two elderly female voices were broken up with static.
"Here Jenny. Pass us one of those Battenbergs would you me old duck?"
Clatter of plates.
"Hang on. Just let me put me choppers in then I can start munching."
Slurping of tea.
Danny and I shot each other a look.
"Told you Shelob was useless," said Danny. "The bloody spider's got the wrong house."
"Perhaps we were expecting too much of Shelob," I said, attempting to smooth things over. "After all, she's only a prototype at this stage. And this was just a dummy run."
Danny held his ground.
"Shelob's useless. Shelob's a loser. The good money's on Boris."

The visuals kicked in displaying two old ladies, one clad in a paisley frock and some fluffy slippers and the other in a pair of pyjamas splattered with cats. The familiar voice of David Attenborough filtered through to the team at the residence of the high commissioner.
"The term biomimesis is a conjoining of two Greek words; bios meaning life, and mimesis – to imitate. An imitation of life. Where art meets engineering. Early notable bio-engineers include Leonardo Da Vinci, with his multitude of sketches of birds and 'flying machines', such as the famous helicopter prototype. Consider the skills and talents of the insect world. In current times, bio-engineers look to bees, cockroaches and dragonflies in order to glean information regarding hive intelligence, resilience and flight respectively. Although the term 'biomimetics' wasn't coined until the 1950s by Otto Schmitt, the concept has been in practice for hundreds of years. Joseph Paxton used the design of a lilypad to structure the Crystal Palace. The Wright brothers modelled their planes on the structure of birds' wings. Georges de Mestral

invented Velcro when he considered how a burr, with its series of tiny hooks, stuck so firmly to his dog's fur. Now a team at Festo have invented a robotic bird."

One of the elderly ladies spoke up.

"Jesus Jenny, I don't believe it. Surely it's not possible. That David Attenborough's gone off the boil, ain't he? Speaking a load of old tut. Robotic birds, my giddy aunt. Whatever next? Robotic spiders?"

A pet tarantula sat in a cage in one corner of the room – a familiar, a pet. The team watched in part anticipation, part horror as Shelob found her way inside the cage and attempted to mate with it.

"Told you Shelob was useless," said Danny, tut-tutting. "Too busy humping to get on with the job. Let's see what Boris is up to."

Boris's audio kicked in. J-I-M, J-I-M – the crew were blaring Jimmy Hendrix. When the visuals were displayed a few minutes later they showed a couple of dreadlocked Africans jiving to the vibe. Boris's visuals were beamed upon the screen.

"Oi," said Gillian. "Boris is heading straight for the booze."

Footage showed a swaying Boris backing out from the liquor cabinet and stumbling drunkenly across the carpet to collapse at the feet of one of the Africans.

"Ha ha," said Gillian. "I told you Boris would amount to nowt. Too busy boozing to keep his mind on the job."

She started up with a resounding if somewhat mocking chorus of an old Who song.

Boris the spider, Boris the spider
Creepy, creepy, crawly, crawly
Creepy, creepy, crawly, crawly

He's come to a sticky end
Don't think he will ever mend
Never more will he crawl 'round
He's embedded in the ground

Boris the spider
Boris the spider

Footage appeared on the screen at the Commissioner's office, showing Jenny passing a joint to Shirley.

"Does wonders for us doesn't it, this ganja – you with your MS and me with my glaucoma."

Gillian gave me a high five.

"Good old Shelob," said Gillian. "I knew she was the spider to back."
Shelob went on to Phase B of the project.

The Glass Screen

In dire need of money, I took the job stripping behind the glass screen. My boyfriend Karl was very much against it. He thought that I was lowering myself by taking up that sort of work. I was an extra-mural student, studying psychology at Massey University, living in London, struggling to get by. I was an illegal immigrant, so there were only a small number of jobs I could take, as I had to be paid under the table. I had flown into Paris from Auckland, made my way to the coast of France and taken a boat across to Blighty, coming ashore in the dead of night.

The stripping job had been advertised in the local paper:

WANTED: WOMEN TO DANCE IN PEEP SHOW. ALL HAIR COLOURS CONSIDERED – BRUNETTE, BLONDE, REDHEAD. CALL BARRY ON 0784 661 0148 .

I called up Barry. He asked if I had any dancing experience.
"Just boogeying with my girlfriends at the weekend," I truthfully replied.

"Well, come on down to the parlour at noon tomorrow and we'll see if we can hook you up," he said.
He gave me the address and hung up.

At midday the following day I made my way down to the parlour. The front door was unlocked. I pushed it open and entered the building. I approached the receptionist and asked for Barry.
"Barry, Barry", she hollered. "There's a lady here to see you."
A man dressed in paint-splattered jeans and a red T-shirt came sauntering out to meet me. He extended his hand in greeting.
"Hi, I'm Barry", he said.
"I'm Katy," I replied.
"Let me show you the dancing booths and then we can have a wee chat," he said.

I followed him through the reception area to the booths, which were glass on one side to enable the gentlemen to peep through at the ladies dancing within.

"You'll be dancing in one of these," he said. "I pay a flat hourly rate and then you'll get ten percent of whatever tips the men leave. Some of the men can be quite generous. You'd be surprised."

"What's the hourly rate?"

"Ten pounds fifty cash in hand. Under the table."

"Okay I'll take the job. When can I start?"

"Tomorrow. There's two shifts, a lunchtime and an evening one. Which would you prefer to work?"

"Can I work both?"

"If you like."

"I'll do that then."

"Before we offer you the job we need a dancing demo."

I shook my booty for a minute or two. He seemed satisfied and said he'd see me at nine the following morning.

I had been working at the peep show for about a month when I noticed that one of the customers kept returning on an all-too-regular basis. Did I have a stalker? The thought freaked me out a bit; but at the same time I was a little flattered that somebody thought me attractive enough to stalk.

He had been haunting me for several weeks when, leaving the parlour one night, I heard grunts and yells coming from an alley to the right. I moved to investigate and, heading into the alley, saw my stalker lying on the ground being beaten to a pulp by two beefcakes in dark-blue jeans and black leather jackets. As they turned towards me I caught a glimpse of their faces. I wanted to help but my legs were frozen solid. I stayed where I was and watched helplessly as the two men pummelled the stalker to death and then ran out past me and jumped into a car that was parked in the street adjoining the alley. Who could I turn to, who could I tell about what I had seen? As an illegal immigrant, I couldn't run to the cops. I trudged home and telephoned Karl. He picked up on the third ring.

"Hello, Karl speaking."

"Jesus Christ, you'll never guess what I just saw."

"What?"

"You know how I've taken a job in the peep show."

"Yeah."

"Well, there's this guy who keeps coming back. Bit of a stalker. Anyway, I was heading home from work when I saw him getting beaten to death in an alley."

"No way. Man I *told* you not to take that job. There's been nothing but trouble since you started."

"Oh, don't be so melodramatic. This is the first incident."

"You know I don't want you stripping."

"That's not the point. The point is that I just saw a man being killed."

"And what do you want me to do about it?"

"You could call the cops and tell them. Say it was you who saw it."

"I'm not going to lie to the cops. I could get in big trouble."

"Well somebody has to tell the police. There's a dead body lying in an alley by the strip club and nobody's been alerted."

"Oh someone will stumble across it at some stage. Just leave it there."

"Fat lot of good you are."

"Why is it up to you to draw attention to a dead stalker?"

"I dunno. I guess I just feel responsible somehow. Almost as if I knew him personally."

"Listen. I really think you need to get some rest. Why don't you put down the phone, have a hot bath and get a decent night's sleep. It'll all look clearer in the morning."

I hung up with a sigh. I did as I was told; drew the bath, climbed in between clean sheets and did my best to head off to the land of nod. But the image of the dead man was sharp in my mind – I couldn't rid myself of it.

I woke up in the morning with dead man images still in my mind. I walked into the kitchen, made myself a coffee, put a tab of Equal into it – (I had gone off sugar to lose weight) and sat down at the table. Somebody would have found the body by now, I reasoned, but thought I had better go back to the alley to check.

I dressed casually in dark-blue jeans and a black turtleneck sweater, my glasses pressed firmly onto my face. I made my way back to the alley. The body was gone. I turned on my heels and was heading back to the street when somebody grabbed me from behind. I squirmed and tried to get away but they held me fast. I was dragged into a car; my feet and hands were bound with rope and a gag was placed over my mouth. There was nothing I could do. I closed my eyes and did not open them again until we reached our destination.

It was a spacious house in the country surrounded by fragrant pines. The rope that bound my legs was untied and I was led into the house. The gag was removed from my mouth.

"Let me go you bloody bastards," I yelled, but they didn't.

They sat me down in a kitchen chair. I heard the front door being locked.

"Tell us what you saw last night in the alley," they demanded, but I refused to answer.

They gestured that I should rise to my feet, so I did. They led me down the hallway past a series of doors, each with a window in it. Every window had a female face pushed up to the pane; prisoners trapped within. They opened up a door and pushed me inside. They smeared red lipstick on my mouth. Applied kohl to my eyes.

"Come on bitch, dance," said one of them. "You wanted to be a stripper, so strip."

They moved round to the other side of the door and watched me through the glass pane. I obeyed their instructions. I swayed from side to side, slowly removing each item of clothing until I danced naked. I heard the men on the other side of the glass slowly applauding. In one corner of the floor rested a single mattress. I dressed myself and lay down.

I had just begun to drift off to sleep when I heard a tapping from the other side of the wall. I climbed out of bed and walked across to it. There was a hole in the wood. I put my eye up to the hole. A wide violet eye looked back at me.

"Hey you," I hissed. "What's your name?"

"June. And you?"

"Katy. How long have you been in here?"

"About three months, I think, but I'm losing track of the days."

"And how did you end up in here? Did they kidnap you too?"

"Yea, I was walking home from my job in a strip joint, when they grabbed me. I think you'll find it's the same for all the women in here."

"And what about the men that perv in at us? What's the story there?"

"Well, the boss of this place is Henry. He's the big fat guy with the man boobs. He runs this place along with a couple of his mates. It's an underground operation. Local men pay top dollar for the privilege of coming here and watching us strip."

"Creepy."

"Yea, but is it really any worse than the lives we led before?"

"*Yes*, it's way worse. Before we were free. Now we're prisoners."

"Yea, but at least we're fed regularly. I was struggling to scrape together enough money for groceries when I was on the outside. And there's regular exercise in the exercise yard. They like us girls to stay fit and healthy."

"Well, it would only take one of us to escape, to liberate all of us."

"How do you mean?"

"If one girl got out she could alert the cops and they could bust this joint."

"Yes, but we're locked in."

"What about the exercise yard? Any way we could go over the wall?"

"No, they watch us like hawks."

"Well, what about befriending one of the guards? Or one of the clients?"

"There is what us girls refer to as Mingling Time, when we go out into the common room in our underwear and meet with the clients. I guess there might be an opportunity for bonding then."

"Exactly. You need to sidle up to one of the clients, make friends. With time he could invite you back to his house. You can alert the local cops and they can come and set the rest of us free."

"Hmm, let me think on it, okay? I'll see you in the exercise yard. Not that we're allowed to talk to one another while we're doing our exercises or anything."

"Okay, see you then."

I lay back down on my mattress, watching a daddy long legs crawl slowly across the ceiling.

At six pm, a plate of food was passed through a flap in the door. Dinner was none too inspiring; an overcooked chicken breast, some watery beans and a dob of mashed potato. I didn't feel like eating, but I ate anyway, I would have to keep my strength up in this place. I wouldn't let the bastards grind me down. After dinner, I pushed the plate back out through the slot, then lay back on the mattress again. Christ, there was nothing to do in this place. The daddy long legs was providing all the excitement. I fell asleep eventually, but it seemed to take forever to head off to the Land of Nod.

At 10 the following morning a bell rang and we were ushered out into the exercise yard. A guard stood at the front, demonstrating the exercises that we were to perform. All of us inmates imitated the guard, left leg forward, left leg back, right leg forward, right leg back. And hush no talking girls, and single file back to your cells.

It was about a month later that June befriended Timothy. They met, as per my suggestion, at Mingling Time. Timothy was standing by himself at the snacks table. June sidled up and started chatting. The following week Timothy started paying extra to be allowed into the room with June as she danced. The week after that, he started paying even more to be June's only customer. He visited her every day for two or three hours. A month or so later he asked our owner if he could be allowed to take June home with him and our owner agreed.

June had been going home with Timothy for about two months when she finally managed to alert the cops. Tim was out doing the gardening; June sneaked to the phone and informed the police that we women were being held prisoner. They came for us in their cars, arrested Henry and his co-workers.

I was booted out of Blighty for being an illegal immigrant. I flew back home to New Zealand, completed my degree, took a job as a psychologist at a local clinic. Images of the underground strip parlour haunted my dreams; at night I was back there, trapped in that room, the walls closing in around me, no possibility of escape.

Cryonics

Jessica

I began my PhD in the summer of 2014. The topic was *Ecology and Genetics of Insect Predators.* I intended to focus on the ladybird, latin name Coccinellidae as I would refer to it in my thesis, and my aim was to develop a renewable pest management system. I chose Stephen as my supervisor because of a fascinating lecture he had given us on predator/ prey relationships and also, as silly as it sounds, he reminded me of my childhood sweetheart, Tom, who had lived next door to me in St Kilda. Stephen had a reputation in the department as being a little 'different'. He kept a uloborid spider in a jar in his office and trapped small insects to feed it. He had made the spider lazy as it did not have to hunt for prey. When I first visited him to discuss my PhD topic Stephen talked mostly about the spider and how it did not use venom on its prey, but instead wrapped its victim in huge amounts of silk, up to 450 feet of it, creating a type of bondage death cocoon. The process takes over an hour and kills by suffocation.

Part of me felt sorry for Stephen because it was common knowledge that his wife had left him to be with her family when she got brain cancer. Rumour had it that she didn't think Stephen was capable of taking care of her properly, which was a slap in the face to Stephen. The word on the street was that Stephen was too preoccupied with his work to look after his wife when she became unwell, that her brain cancer was a serious, a terminal, condition. Some people said he should have taken time off work to look after her and to be with her during her dying days, but I didn't want to pass judgment. The implication was that he only cared about himself and not about others. I felt that people were being too hard on Stephen, and I had noticed the signs of depression in him, the fading eyes and the drooping shoulders and so, when he was my PhD supervisor I worked hard to cheer him up.

I would crack jokes in an effort to make Stephen laugh. Then I started giving him back rubs and things progressed from there. Before I really knew what was happening we were engaged in an ill advised affair. I knew that it wasn't a good idea and could influence my PhD grade, not necessarily in a positive manner. What would happen if the affair came to an end? I knew as well as anybody that these things can turn nasty when they finish, with bitter and acrimonious feelings involved and I did not know how it was going to turn out with Stephen.

My PhD progressed slowly. Piled higher and deeper was right; at times I felt as if I was drowning in research notes. I didn't see my own friends very often while I was seeing Stephen; he didn't like it. He said I should be busy with my PhD and that he could fulfill all my needs. A couple of times, early on in the relationship, I caught him checking my mobile phone. When he saw that I had been texting a friend called Gus he flew through the roof, even though the texts were harmless.

"Gus!" he screeched. "I have never heard of Gus! Tell me who is this Gus that you were texting at 9.57pm at night?"

"Gus is Augustus Marshall", I said. "An old friend from high school. We don't keep in touch that often I just wanted to know how he was doing. He's just started a new job."

"Augustus is it?", he mocked. "Oh fancy, like Augustus Gloop? Bring on the oompa loompas"

He curled his index finger under my chin and brought his face in close to mine.

"Listen sweetheart, I don't want you contacting any strangers, and especially not strange *men*."

"But Gus isn't a stranger, he's…"

"I don't care what you say. He's a stranger to me. You're not to contact him again. I forbid it."

This was a new side to Stephen that I was seeing. Even though it was controlling, I justified his behavior by telling myself that he only did it out of love. He didn't want to lose me. He saw Gus as a threat and he didn't want me to begin an affair. I felt sorry for him. He seemed to really need me. He told me about how his wife had been faking how sick she was as an excuse to skive off her responsibilities. I felt like I needed some space from him so when my friend Sophie asked me out for a girl's night I jumped at the chance. I just needed to go out and forget the intensity of it all. Sophie and I went shopping for some new outfits.

We had a ball. I hadn't hung out with Sophie in ages. We found this great new clothes shop that hadn't been around that long. Trying lots of dresses on I found the one I liked – A light grey colour, tight fitting with an asymmetrical hemline. We indulged in some new makeup too and I brought a new bra. We dined for lunch at the Rave Café and then Sophie and I went our separate ways, planning to catch up later that night at the pub.

I stopped in to see Stephen on the way home. I had dropped off the first draft of my PhD for him to check two weeks earlier. Arriving at the university I ran up the stairs excited to see Stephen. Entering the lab I smiled and gave him a big hug.

"I've been shopping with Sophie." I blurted out. "It was so fun - we brought a new outfit each to go out in tonight."

I pulled the dress out of the bag as I was talking and my new bra fell out too.

His face dropped and darkened. What's this?" He said as he stooped down to pick it up.

"So you are going out with Sophie and you brought a tarty dress and some new lingerie?" He asked accusingly.

"Well, yes." I said quietly the excitement draining out of my body. "We are going to have a girl's night- it was her idea." I added as an afterthought as I sensed his disapproval.

"I don't want you going out with that Sophie." He said "I've seen her around campus and she's always talking to males, flirting, I don't trust her. She's a tart."

Silence reigned. I didn't know what to say.

"Why don't you want to spend all your free time with me?" He continued

"Well it's already been planned." I said quietly.

"What? Speak up girl stop muttering." He answered

I suddenly plucked up some courage why was he treating me like this? I was not a child who needed telling off. He used to be so nice.

"I'm sorry Stephen I'm going." I said.

He shot me a filthy look and turned his back on me. "By the way the latest draft of your PhD was not crash hot maybe you need to spend time doing research rather than hanging out with that tramp." I was offended, Sophie was my friend and she wasn't a tramp I couldn't believe he was jealous now of my girlfriends.

I left the room. I had to get away. I loved him but I felt guilty. Why should I feel guilt?

***

Stephen

Jessica was perfect. She had a perfect body. She had a perfect soul. She had flown through her undergraduate degree with first class Honours. I had noticed her about the department as an undergraduate and had my eye on her, sizing her up. She used to wear tartan mini skirts with high heeled boots and V-neck skivvies in the winter and flowing patterned cotton dresses in the summer. I liked the way she dressed. She stood out from the crowd a little; at least for me.

My wife was becoming even more helpless and demanding. After work I would come home tired expecting things done as they had been done for years. She had always been a dutiful wife. A great cook and a tidy housewife. But now her sickness had made her selfish and lazy. She was lying in bed feeling sorry for herself and whenever I tried to get her up to help me with the mountain of chores that were actually *her* jobs she would just tell me to have more sympathy and to google her sickness

Glioblastoma multiforme. She told me it was a very serious condition that was fatal and would kill her in just a few months. Apparently that's what the specialists had told her the ones she had being seeing for weeks. The ones that had almost drained our bank account from all their fees. They were probably all making it up to make money out of us I didn't believe she was that sick. I'm sure it was just an excuse. I had never gone to the doctors with her even though she had asked me too. I was too busy at work, she should have known that. Also something that she didn't know I was having a fantastic time with Jessica. The sweet naïve young thing - her innocence intrigued me. Her oblivious gullible opinion of me. She was still young enough and inexperienced enough to believe in true love. It was great - she was putty in my hands.

My wife was really beginning to get on my nerves. She was becoming a drain and I did not know how I could care for her. I could not tend to all her needs – she was so demanding. She seemed to want me to do everything for her and would not try to help herself. Sometimes I just wanted her to go to sleep and never wake up. One evening I took some chloroform from the biology lab home with me. I thought I would be doing her a favour by putting her to sleep until such time as a cure for brain cancer had been found. I waited until she was sleeping, then poured chloroform onto a hanky and smothered her nose and face with it. When I was sure she was unconscious (by shaking her to see if she would wake) I wrapped her body in silk, then slung her over my shoulder and carried her downstairs to the deep freeze. I opened the door of the freezer and placed her body inside, then closed the door. She would sleep soundly until it was time to wake up – when a cancer cure had been found. Now I could concentrate on my relationship with Jessica; spend more time with her so she would not want to go out on girl's nights.

I texted Jessica and told her that my wife had gone to France where her family could care for her in her illness. That's what I would tell everybody to avoid suspicion. I thought that Jessica would be happy to hear this as it would mean that we could then be together. Jessica thought that my wife had gone away very suddenly and she pondered why I wasn't actually caring for her.

***

Jessica
A few weeks went by before I informed the authorities about Stephen's wife's disappearance. After the body was found in the freezer, there was a lengthy investigation and trial, the upshot of which was that Stephen was ordered to a psychiatric institution for an indeterminate length of time, rather than being given a fixed jail sentence. He was sectioned

under an inpatient compulsory treatment order. He wasn't happy about it.

"At least a jail term has an end date", he complained.

They sent him to Hillmorton. The first treatment order was extended to a second after Stephen played up and did not do as he was told in hospital where the staff liked everybody to follow orders, nice and obedient, then the second order was extended into a third indefinite one. It looked like he would be in there for the rest of his life.

We wrote letters to each other and I tried to cheer him up and tell him that the end could be in sight, but he thought I was just feeding him false hope. They had locked him in seclusion or solitary confinement after he had lost control and thrown a chair at a nurse. It went without saying that he hated the place and could not wait to get out. I encouraged him to make his room nice so that he would have a sanctuary in that pit of hell and sent him postcards and posters he could pin to the walls. I still had feelings for Stephen, even though I knew he had murdered his wife. I knew that in his own mind, his actions had been justified and he had thought that he was just putting her to sleep for a spell of time until a cure for brain cancer could be found. In his scientific eagerness, in his absentmindedness, he had overlooked the fact that the deep freeze could actually kill her. Or had he? This was the fact that the jury had debated for hours and eventually they had decided that a man of Stephen's intelligence should definitely have foreseen that his actions could lead to his wife's death. However, after Stephen's performance in the courtroom, they had not been convinced of his sanity and had decided to send him to Hillmorton.

I visited him just twice. I was not sure if the nurses would let me through to his room but they did. The first time I visited was after he'd been in there a year. We had been writing letters to each other and Stephen, who could be persuasive, convinced me to go and visit him.

I perched awkwardly on the end of the bed and tried to make small talk about movies I had been to see, when in reality I was fighting back the tears, seeing Stephen in this reduced state. He was drugged up to the eyeballs and could hardly speak. He had gained an enormous amount of weight and carried a psychotropic beer belly that hung out over his pyjama bottoms and wore a sad looking pair of worn out fluffy bunny slippers on his feet that made him look like a jaded clown. I asked him what medications they had him on but he said he couldn't remember. He asked about the spider right away and I said I had been looking after it properly and feeding it hefty doses of insects each day. I told him that it was looking fat and healthy and was thriving in its new environment. He seemed happy with this news. He said he didn't think they were ever going to set him free, that he thought he would never see the outside world again, and that he consoled himself with small walks around the courtyard, sometimes picking flowers, daffodils and jonquils from the garden to take back to his room.

"I never intended to kill her", he said, looking me straight in the eye. "It was an accident. That's why I think my punishment is too over the top. That's why I get angry at the staff here. I don't see that justice is being done. I'm sick of being treated like a little child. Locked away forever from society. Labelled dangerous – a big sticker stuck to my forehead. I'm sick of being labelled. My career is ruined. Even if I did get out, I'd never find work again. I wish I'd never met my wife, then none of this would have happened. I'm not saying there weren't good times, but look at what the relationship led to in the end. The destruction of both of us."

I tried my best to console him. I reached out and stroked his hair, then brought his head in close to my chest.

"Remember the good times", I said. "I've seen the photos of the two of you together taking a cycling tour across Europe when you were young, having picnics in the park, sailing on the Rhine. It all looks so romantic, the early days of your marriage. The golden years. People would pay good money to have those memories."

"It's all been tainted", he said negatively.

"It's just your frame of mind", I said. "You're down in the dumps from being stuck in this place and who wouldn't be? Perhaps I can help you get into meditation. I'll send a tape."

He scoffed.

"You'll have me into yoga next! No, I just make myself content with my daily ambles and my nonsensical conversations with the other inmates. One of them's a maestro on the piano. If you stick around you might get to hear her bash out a tune."

It was nearly lunchtime and something slightly manic in Stephen's demeanour was beginning to make me feel uncomfortable. I excused myself and said that I had to get to Canterbury University to catch up with another lecturer who was teaching on a similar topic to me. I had landed a job as a junior lecturer after completing my PhD. Stephen's trial had taken place before he'd finished supervising me, so I'd had to change supervisors and had finished up under the tutelage of Philip Watson who did a good job of helping me see the project through to its conclusion.

It was six months later when I visited Stephen again. We had continued to write to each other. In some of his letters he had professed his love and signed off with kisses. I hadn't reciprocated, but I still felt that I should visit him as his was no doubt an odd and lonely life, locked away in Hillmorton for a crime he professed not to mean to commit. It was an overcast day; drizzle fell from the sky, coating everything in a fine spray. I had made the drive up from Dunedin the night before and was staying in a small unit at the Bella Vista motel. It wasn't fancy but it was practical, clean and tidy and it suited me fine. I dressed in a simple navy wool suit to keep out the winter chill and topped it off with a woolen hat which had been a gift from my aunt. I drove to Hillmorton, parked in the carpark and walked briskly to the entrance. A nurse greeted me at the door.

"Hello, can I help you?" she asked in an authoritative tone.

"I'm here to see Stephen Barker", I said.

"And you are?"

"Gillian Miles. A friend."

"Alright", she said in an icy tone. "Come through."

I met Stephen in the hallway. He carried something in his arms – I could not see what it was. As I drew closer I saw that it was a length of fabric. He laid it on the ground and encouraged me to lie down on it.

"Won't you lie down on this beautiful silk and rest your tired body a while?"

The Accidental Time Travelers

Julian flew through all the tests we sat at the Lyndon B. Johnson Space Center in Houston, Texas. He had a first in physics from Harvard. He was top of our class and so attracted envy. He didn't vomit in the KC-135 also known as the Weightless Wonder or 'Vomit Comet'. He was a champion in the Neutral Buoyancy Lab, had no trouble staying under water for seven hours at a time. He was great in the cockpit of a T-38, soaring through the heavens like an angel or a god. He took like a duck to Russian and was fluent within a month. It was sickening. He was the golden boy; he shone. He was my best friend, but I must admit that at times I fell prey to the sin of envy where Julian was concerned. It was difficult not to.

Cynthia trained in the year behind us. I had a crush on her from the moment I laid eyes on her. She had shoulder length wavy dark brown hair and green eyes, like a cat, eyes that seemed to see right through you and know all your secrets, know you inside out, even though you had only just met. Cynthia was special to me from the start. I tried hard to hide my feelings, but I'm sure I blushed a few times when she talked to me. Cynthia was average at Nasa, which still meant she was a superstar in the real world, because standards were set so high. She was diligent and passed all her tests with ease, but she was not in Julian's league. To be fair, nobody was.

As for me I had a Masters degree in Computer Science from Yale, gained in 2030, and had worked for three years at IBM. I threw up in the vomit comet and could only stay three hours underwater in the Neutral Buoyancy Lab, but to my surprise they passed me and I became a qualified astronaut.

The three of us were chosen to venture together into outer space on SS Celestial. When I heard that Cynthia was going to be on the journey with me, living in close quarters, I got nervous. Would she see me getting undressed? Would she hear me snore? It would be make or break with the two of us living together in space. The mission should we choose to accept it? To head to Mars to look for water and to bring back samples of the planet's surface for study. Part of the assignment was also to look for signs of life. The mission was our first. We were excited about the trip. Julian went especially quiet in the days leading up to our departure, his genius mind ticking over with thoughts I would never know.

The preparation was intense. We attended several seminars leading up to the departure date prepping us for our mission on Mars. The ship was stocked with everything we would need and more, our suits were fitted and we were sent home for two days to rest.

On the day of departure, we had to be at base by 4am ready for a 7am takeoff. When I arrived, Cynthia was already there but no sign of Julian. He arrived at 4 30am looking as though he hadn't slept in days, unnaturally silent and looking somber.

We went over our flight briefing with the ground crew and embarked onto the ship. Butterflies danced in my stomach - we were actually doing it! This is what I had dreamed of since I was a little boy, now the dream had become a reality.

We were strapped into our seats and the countdown on the screen appeared. Taking off was the most amazing feeling I had ever experienced; the velocity glued me to the back of my seat.

Once we had ascended into space we were able to take our belts off, zero gravity had taken effect. The view was wonderful, just like I had imagined it would be. We managed to see planet earth in the distance as well as the moon and the sun. I noticed Cynthia looked awestruck as she sat staring out the window.

The first few days passed without anything notable to report back to base, communication with ground crew was frequent. We passed the time by playing Agricola, Catan, and chess in the simulated gravity room. The food wasn't great and was mostly freeze – dried, heated up by a microwave. There were six of us in total on the ship; Julian, Cynthia and me along with James, who was always clowning around, and who had been assigned the job of looking for water along with Natalie, and Steven whose job it was to gather samples of the planet's surface with me. Julian and Cynthia had been assigned the task of looking for signs of life. Julian was prone to dark moods. I hadn't known that about him although I had never lived with him before. I wondered if the confinement was getting to him. It was hard living with six others in such close quarters.

Cynthia and I seemed to get along the best and I wondered how long it would be before we became a romantic item - the thought made my spine tingle. She was so beautiful and graceful even in space.

Everything was going well until day thirty-six. It started off as a normal day with coffee and muesli for breakfast. Julian appeared to be in one of his moods again, not talking to anyone and avoiding eye contact as he obsessed over his folder of notes, flicking over the pages in an aggressive manner. We all set about getting on with our day except Julian who stood staring out the main window. I was right behind him when it happened. I heard a low guttural noise escape from Julian's throat. I looked at him as his body tensed in what I first thought was the beginning of some sort of seizure. My thoughts on this were wrong as just then Julian spun around declaring loudly "Holy shit, we're in the path of a meteor shower."

I looked out the window in shock, but my shock dwindled as I saw only empty space.

"What are you talking about? Everything's fine." I said

"Everything's not bloody fine." He snapped back at me. "Can't you see those rocks? We are going to hit them!"

Shit I thought to myself Julian, our captain, was losing it.

I was second in charge, it would be up to me to drive the ship if Julian wasn't coping with reality.

I had to think fast "Come on Julian," I said. "I'll make you a cup of tea."

He looked at me and something in his eyes sent red flags frantically flapping in my mind.

"We have to divert off course." Julian yelped. It was then that he lunged for the Hyperspace button smashing the plastic so fast that I didn't even have time to intervene. The Hyperspace button was special and hidden behind a plastic screen. We had been warned not to touch unless we were about to hit something such as a meteor or a planet, as it would detour the ship off course.

"Julian! No!" I gasped.

But it was too late - he pushed that damned button down so quickly and the ship accelerated faster than the speed of light and we were off to a new random destination in space-time.

***

The ship slowed down when it reached the atmosphere of the new planet which we came to call Solaria 74. Julian was senseless, muttering to himself about the pressure of being Number One and I could not gain control of the ship, so we crash landed. The surface of the planet was light pink and dusty – the color of flamingoes. We tried to communicate with earth but the communications system was broken. I asked the ship what year it was – fortunately one of the ship's computers had survived the crash and announced that it was the year 2065, thirty years into the future. Cynthia and I stepped out nervously, holding hands, onto the terrain that stretched out before us. The others followed, all except Julian who was still catatonic on board. We could see for miles – the dust was only knee high. The air was clear and bright. It was very hot and looking up I could see three suns burning in the sky. Golden dust fell from the suns towards the planet's surface. No inhabitants were to be seen. After talking amongst ourselves, we agreed to set out walking, in search of life.

Twenty minutes into our trek, we came across a small pool of water in the ground which Cynthia said was a promising sign.

"Where there's water, there's life", she said optimistically.

We had been walking for an hour and a half across a dusty pink landscape when we saw the first burrow. It rose up about six-foot above the ground and appeared to be made from a form of yellow mud brick.

"Hey," exclaimed Cynthia. "That looks like a form of housing."

We all got very excited. Although we were baking, we started running towards the burrow. We were about ten meters away when a strange creature, in a lobster-like shell, about one and a half times the size of a human emerged from the burrow and started scuttling towards us.

"Look," I said. "Life!"

The others pulled in close behind me. No one said a thing we all froze, and just watched. The creature came about a meter in front of us and started opening and shutting its mandibles.

"Oh my god," said Cynthia, pulling her body close to mine. "Is it going to eat us?"

"C'mon let's be brave," I said, with a false courage I did not feel. The creature just stood staring at us as we stared at it. I approached it somewhat fearfully and extended my hand. It continued to stare at us without any movement or sound and did not take up my offer of a handshake.

It then turned and scuttled away glancing back at us as it disappeared back into its burrow.

We didn't follow it. We were satisfied that it seemed harmless. We continued walking until we came to more burrows that were larger surrounding what looked like a town center as it had something that looked like a monument in the middle.

We sat down on the monument steps to work out a plan. I thought we should go back and check on Julian to make sure he was okay, **the others agreed.**

Once back at the ship, Julian seemed calmer and I wondered if he had taken one of the valium that were stashed in the first aid kit. We told him everything we had just seen including the strange creature and a description of its shell.

"I've ventured outside," answered Julian "This place has three suns, so it makes sense that the creature you saw had what sounds like an exoskeleton that would protect it from the harsh rays. We will have to make sure we wear our space suits and helmets when we are outside to protect us too."

"How the hell are we going to get back to earth?" Cynthia said in a slight panicked voice. "According to the ship's computer we're thirty years into the future."

"Well I can confirm that the ship is well and truly stuffed," chanted Julian.

We sat talking until the suns went down and two moons appeared. We decided to sleep on the problem of how to get back to earth and attempt to devise a plan in the morning.

I couldn't sleep well that first night, I don't think any of us did as we all looked shattered in the morning. We had a talk and it was decided we would have to try make friends with the inhabitants of this planet if we were to survive. I suggested that we approach the creature we had seen in the first burrow that we had come across as it had already seen us. The others agreed.

So next thing you know we found ourselves tentatively walking towards the creature's burrow. Before we got to the door it came out as though expecting us, gesturing for us to follow it back inside. We all looked at each other and nodded in agreement.

Once inside, I noticed that rough windows had been carved into the walls to let in the daylight. The inside walls were lined with something that looked like cotton wool, and which I was later to learn was the inside of the pod of a plant that resembled a giant bean. The burrow was divided into four with rudimentary walls. The creature communicated with squeaking sounds, grunts and hand gestures and we gestured back. It seemed friendly enough and did not try to attack or eat us. It introduced us to others of its kind – we met about ten at first and some others later. We named our new friend Abelon. He became our guide and taught us how to harvest a local fruit that was a lot like a banana passionfruit, only bigger, how to chop off and boil to eat shoots that resembled supplejack, and he also taught us how to hunt a creature that looked like a cross between a giant porcupine and a crab – with a hard shell and a snout with which it sought out food.

Sixty days into our new life Julian began responding to voices that weren't there. They weren't too dramatic – they didn't tell him to kill or steal, they just told him that he was in immediate danger and that his friends were his enemies. He became extremely paranoid. I sat him down with a cup of tea and he confessed to me that he was a diagnosed schizophrenic but that he'd had to hide this from everybody as Nasa never would have let him in with a mental health history.

"Everybody thinks I'm such a golden boy", he said. "They don't know how troubled I really am. I was diagnosed with schizophrenia when I was twenty-two but I didn't let on to Nasa. I had to go off medication to pass the drugs test. It's been hell. I went back on the meds for this trip but now I've run out. I'm okay when there's a really strict routine and everything goes according to plan. I'm good when I'm kept busy all the time, but any break in structure can be dangerous for me. I've had to keep this hidden and the pressure of keeping it hidden has been intense. Imagine if Nasa knew! I'd be out on the street."

What could I say? Nasa's policies allowed no room for mental illness, not even in very bright candidates like Julian. There was no room, no time for nervous breakdowns and crack ups, probably because, as Julian had proven, they were so dangerous when they happened on a space ship. They wanted well rounded, mentally balanced candidates, not unbalanced geniuses. After all, it was because of Julian that we were now on this planet with no way to get home, stranded far from Planet Earth, having to make do as best we could. I was a bit angry with him for not being honest about his condition, but I felt sorry for him as well. Now we were on this distant planet somewhere in the galaxy and he had run out of psychiatric medication. Great!

***

It was tragic when we found him – the hunting spear through his throat. I couldn't help but think that if he'd been honest with everybody about his illness somebody could have got some more assistance for him. Perhaps covering it all up had been his downfall – trying to be perfect, trying to be number one all the time – it was all just an act. He was hiding deep psychological flaws.

And so, we settled into life on this strange new planet – minus Julian. We had no choice, we were stuck here. We made the best of it, eating local flora and fauna, dining like locals and we grew friendly with some of the local inhabitants. The relationship between Cynthia and I blossomed and we became an item, bonded through our unusual experiences, brought together by adversity. We adjusted to this odd way of existence and even grew to quite like it.

People can adapt to anything given time.

The Scarecrow

They had me written off for dead. They found me in the field behind Kev Thompson's place, my eyes wide open, staring at the sun, my mouth hanging open, slack-jawed. It was a group of skin heads that did me over – I must have looked at them the wrong way, next thing I knew they attacked me down a Christchurch city alleyway, did me over good. They drove with my body out to a farm on the outskirts of the city and dumped me. I was found the next morning by Kevin, the farmer.

He drove with me to the nearest A&E which was located at St George's Hospital. I was patched up and sent back out to face the world after being kept in overnight for observation. In their cruelty, they had beaten me violently around the head with an iron bar and when I went back to my old life, I noticed that I suffered short term memory loss. I worked as an usher at the local theatre, but I took three months off work to recover. I joined the local brain injury support group and thanked my lucky stars when I saw some of the members – perhaps I had gotten off lightly. Some of the group's members could not walk or talk – those were mostly the car crash victims. We also had a couple of people who'd had brain tumours removed and another man who had been beaten up. We used to meet for coffees, pumpkin and chocolate chip muffins and chat at the Dux de Lux each Thursday.

I did exercises to improve my memory – sudoku and luminosity. I also utilised mnemonic devices.

I ate a lot of fish and fresh fruit and vegetables and consumed vitamins B, C, E and Omega-3 fish oil supplements. I did all I could to help myself. I did not smoke or drink. I lived the life of a saint. I treated my brain as a precious commodity. I could not afford to damage any more of its cells.

I met Molly through the brain injury support group. She'd had an astrocytoma brain tumour removed the previous spring and although the operation had gone smoothly it had still been scary. She'd had to learn how to walk again, with the aid of a physiotherapist. She still couldn't run. I took her on a date to the movies – I got free tickets. We went to see This Beautiful Fantastic – a British romantic drama. I took her hand half an hour into the film. She squeezed my hand tightly which I took to be a good sign.

The doctor had told me not to drive, but I hated not having my independence, so I was driving Molly home from the film along a dark Christchurch back road to her flat. Molly got a bit frisky on the way home and unzipped my trousers. I got a bit excited and didn't mind my driving like perhaps I should have. I veered off the road – there was an awful thump; something heavy bounced off the bonnet and then the windscreen. O God what had I hit, a sheep? A dog?

I stopped the car told Molly to stay put and went out to investigate. The headlights were still on so I could clearly see what I had hit. It was a man. I rushed over he was lying so still. I bent down to hear if he was still breathing and could smell the overwhelming odour of alcohol. I panicked - I had hit a person!

"We hit him, it's our fault, we could go to jail." I jumped and turned Molly had gotten out of the car and was standing behind me. Her face registered shock and she was shaking. I stared at her not knowing what to say or do. She stared back at me then suddenly burst into tears, sobbing uncontrollably.

"Don't worry." I squeaked. Surprised at my strained voice I cleared my throat. I think he's dead but I'll call an ambulance.

"No." she retorted back at me "We can't involve the authorities, it was my fault I was distracting you, I'll get into trouble. We will both get into trouble. We'll go to jail!"

"What are we going to do then?" I said "We can't just leave him here."

"We need to dispose of the body," she whispered back at me looking around as she did so as if there might be ears around to hear her outrageous idea.

"C'mon help me," she said bending over the body and grabbing the dead man's shoulders.

I was in shock - I didn't know what to do. I felt I wasn't in control of my body at that moment let alone my mind. I found myself mechanically moving and bending down to pick up his legs. We carried him to the car, placed him in the back seat in a lying down position, and got into the front seats. We drove without speaking. I had given up thinking of what to do I was just following Molly's orders on autopilot. We approached the Rakaia Bridge. Molly told me to stop, so I did.

Next thing you know we were dragging the body out of the back seat and hurling it over the edge of the bridge.

I drove Molly home in silence. Dropped her back at her flat and told her I hoped she could sleep ok after what we had done.

"I'll be ok," she said "I have some sleeping pills."

The body washed up six weeks later. There were news reports on TV and the radio. Molly and I argued about whether to confess or not. I wanted to come clean, she didn't.

"We could be had on manslaughter or even murder charges", said Molly. "Your doctor and the DVLA had told you not to drive and you were driving. I was distracting you. It doesn't look good. We didn't own up at the time. We tried to cover up. It'll look terrible in court."

The guilt started to get to us. I jumped at every knock at the door, imagining it to be a policeman come to handcuff me and take me away, and then the nightmares started up. They were terrible dark dreams where I was buried alive next to the man we had killed, locked in the coffin with him, unable to break free.

Somebody dobbed us in. As it turns out somebody had seen our car stopped at the edge of the Rakaia Bridge and thought it odd and noted down our licence plate number in case something fishy was going on. Bloody snoops. We got ten years each – the judge said our brain injuries were a mitigating factor or it would have been longer. She served her sentence in Arohata Prison in Tawa, I did time at Christchurch Men's. We wrote longing love letters to each other from our cells, told each other to keep thinking of our release date, that glorious day in the future when we would have served our sentence and would be set free – free to roam planet earth once more, free to shop and cook and take delight in each other, free to console one another over our injuries, free to smile and understand.

The Cellar

When we found Sam he weighed only 14 kilos and was non verbal. It was very difficult to communicate with him. If you got too close to him he would bite. I didn't blame him for his aggression. He'd been locked in his parents' cellar for 3 years, with minimal food, sometimes eating rats he'd caught with his bare hands. He was six years old when I found him. By this stage he was more animal than human. His primal instincts had developed but he had not developed speech and he was not toilet trained. He soiled himself regularly – it was me who cleaned up the mess. I got him into nappies and tried to teach him to use the toilet. I was a social worker who had been assigned the case. It had been me who had found him, curled up in a ball, chained to the wall, with skinny limbs, a bloated tummy and burn marks on him. His hair was matted and dirty and full of nits. The boss had assigned me the case to test whether or not I was ready for promotion. I was determined to do a good job.

My name was Sally and I had a real passion for child protection because of what I had lived through in my childhood. My mother used to drag me around by the hair and put me in baths that were either boiling hot or freezing cold. I used to get terrible carpet burns I had to hide from the other kids at school. She used to have a 'Time Out' room she would lock me in if I 'misbehaved'. If I accidentally broke something, ate food from the fridge because I was hungry or got up too early and woke her up she would shove me in Time Out and lock the door, trapping me in there. I never knew how long I would be in there for or what I had to do to be let out. So when the boss assigned me Sam's case I felt that I could make a major difference in one boy's life, help shape the course of his destiny.

It was one of the neighbours who alerted social welfare to the case. They had heard screams coming from the direction of the cellar and seen the parents going down there with vegetable scraps. Once I been assigned the case, I drove to the address at around 10pm at night. I did not want to alert the parents to my presence as I knew they would deny all abuse and would try and stop me from saving the boy. I crept around the side of the house with a flashlight and a blanket, and found the cellar door. It was locked. Knowing that this would probably be the case, I had thought ahead and had bought bolt cutters with me. I snipped through the lock and pushed open the door. A soft whimpering came from one corner. I walked in the direction of the noise and saw a small boy curled up in the foetal position on a cardboard box. From where I stood I could see what looked like burn marks on his skin.

I took a deep breath and walked towards him, holding out my hand in what I thought was a friendly gesture. As soon as I got close to him, he bit my hand, drawing blood. I remained calm and tried to speak soothing words. I had to get him out of here and into the car. I moved behind him and wrapped the blanket around his shoulders, picking him up in my arms. He thrashed and resisted at first, but I stroked his back and he relaxed a little and let me carry him out to the car. I didn't even know if he understood English but I kept talking to him.

"It's going to be okay", I said. "Everything's going to turn out fine now. You've been rescued."

He made no reply. I put him in the back seat and put the kiddie locks on, then started driving to the nearest place that could tend to his wounds, Mercy Hospital. Some of those burns looked pretty bad.

I arrived at the hospital twenty minutes later and walked through the sliding doors into A&E. I approached the counter.

"Hello", I said. "I've got a young boy here who's been severely neglected and abused. He has burns that need tending to. Is there somebody who can take care of this."

"Name?" asked the nurse, rather abruptly, given the circumstances.

"My name is Sally Roberston. I'm not sure of the boy's first name, but he belongs to the Phillips household."

The office had done some checks on the family before sending me around. The parents were P addicts on the dole. The father had been in jail for drug dealing. We lifted the boy up onto the bed. The doctor came in to look at him. He declared that the boy had malnutrition, a severe case of head lice, infected burn wounds, rotten teeth and was severely underweight. They wanted to keep him in overnight to give him IV fluids and I agreed that this should be the case. They told me they were going to shave his head to get rid of the lice and give him antibiotics and that he might have to be put under to get his teeth removed. The doctor gave the boy a sedative as he seemed very anxious. I gave them my details and told them to ring me the next day. I asked to go and see the boy before I left. They said he might be a bit drowsy from the sedative but that I could have five minutes with him. I entered the room, the little soul looked so small in the big hospital bed, his eyes half closed. I took his hand and he flinched. I told him to stay strong, that he was in good care and that I would come and see him tomorrow.

I didn't sleep a wink that night, thinking about the poor boy. On the way home I stopped in at the local Farmers and bought him a complete new set of clothes – a Superman T-shirt, a nice pair of jeans and a hoodie plus some underwear. I called by the hospital on the way to work and found my young charge sipping a cold drink through a straw. It was noticeable the amount of teeth that were missing – when he opened his mouth I could see huge gaps; he had obviously had a number of teeth extracted. A smile came to his face when he saw the clothes. His eyes darted nervously towards the door, perhaps wondering if his parents would show up. It would take a while for him to learn to trust me because it was an exceptionally bad abuse case.

Later that afternoon I went around to see the parents with the police. We walked up the weed strewn path. Bottles of Woodstock littered the front porch. One of the cops knocked on the door. A woman answered. Her appearance was a shock, she was incredibly thin, still in her nightgown even though it was the afternoon, her eyes glazed and her stance wobbly.

"What do you want?" She snapped

"We are here to talk to you about your son." Replied one of the cops

"I don't have a son." She said, her stance immediately becoming defensive. Attempting to shut the door. The cop reacted fast and stuck his foot in the door to prevent it from closing.

"We need to take you and your husband to the station to ask you a few questions." Said the cop

"Bill!" screamed the woman "The bloody coppers are here!"

An equally disheveled man appeared behind the woman.

"Whats going on?" Asked the man "We done nuthin wrong."

The cop managed to talk them into getting into the police car with minimal fuss and I followed behind in my car.

Once at the station I wasn't permitted to be in the interview room but I stuck around anyway.

I was told that the parents denied everything at first but then succumbed to the interrogation and charges were being pressed. They would appear in court this Friday and I could go along if I wanted.

I was also told that they had been in touch with the boy's Aunt and Uncle and that they had agreed to take the boy in. I was given their details and appointed as the boy's social worker to oversee his care.

Two days later I picked the boy up from hospital. He was wearing his new clothes I had brought him. I put him into the back seat of my car. I talked to him on the way asking him his name but he didn't reply; he looked like he was in shock.

Arriving at his Aunt's & Uncle's address the house looked well kept in a nice neighbourhood. Knocking on the door a man answered. Looking at the boy he frowned and said abruptly,

"Who's this ragamuffin?"

I replied "He's your nephew the police contacted you the other day and you agreed to take him in as he has been neglected and abused by his parents, your brother."

"Hey Beryl!" the man called over his shoulder. A woman appeared "D

Goes around with the police to see the parents. Press charges, parents go to jail.

They send him to live with an uncle but he does not get looked after properly. In the end social worker adopts him.

In the end, I adopted him. I thought it best. How else was I going to ensure he was properly looked after? I tended to him with a motherly love. I taught him to read and write, and tamed his nature which, after all the abuse, had become savage.

The Roofer

I haven't been homeless all my life. There was a time when I had a cozy bed to sleep in and a fine roof over my head. Hello my name is Stefan Stevenson. Before finding myself homeless, I worked at Siam Commercial Bank but was not very high up there. I was only twenty-three, had recently completed my degree in Economics and was just starting out in my career. I had lived at home during my degree in order to save money, and upon coming out from New Zealand to Phuket to work had found myself awfully lonely.

Women were my downfall. One woman in particular. Fern was her name and she had been born in Phuket which was where I was living when I lost my apartment. I met her in a bar and we chatted the whole night. She told me her last name but did not give me her phone number. I looked her up on Facebook the next day and sent her a message during working hours the following day. Very soon we were chatting away, day and night, both in and out of worktime and it wasn't long before I was called in front of the boss and asked about my decreased productivity. I had gotten so engrossed in my conversations with Fern, so carried away with the moment, I had forgotten about the CCTV cameras that dotted the inside of the building. Management were able to monitor what employees were doing on their computers during worktime. I realised the messages I had prided myself on being so private were actually public property. No doubt the bulk of them had been seen by management, which was more than embarrassing as some of them were quite sexually suggestive. I was in deep trouble.

Confronted by management, I panicked and stuttered. This was my first job since graduation and I hadn't intended to make a mess of it - I wanted a good reference. It was simply that I had got too involved too quickly with Fern. We didn't have an actual relationship. Not only had we not slept together, we hadn't even kissed. Since that night in the bar, I'd not plucked up the courage to ask her out on a date, being quintessentially shy, and our relationship had been limited to and defined by Facebook. Emoticons littered our chats. I sent her exploding hearts - in return she sent me virtual flowers. It was sweet, and harmless. Or was it? Here I was, about to lose my job if I wasn't careful, all because of a virtual relationship with a woman I had met only once.

The boss told me he knew I was using Facebook during working hours and that this was a big no-no. He gave me a written warning and told me if he caught me using the application again at work I would be fired on the spot, no time for excuses. I thanked him for the second chance and went back to my desk feeling much subdued.

That evening, I explained to Fern what had happened. I told her I couldn't contact her during working hours anymore and our relationship had to be limited to after hours. She agreed – she told me my job was important and she didn't want me to lose it because of her. I thanked her for being so understanding and rang off the phone feeling a little better. At least Fern had been compassionate. Some women would have sulked or thrown a tantrum at the thought of the loss of communication, but Fern had handled the situation with grace. It made me like her even more.

I ran a hot bath and soaked my tired body for forty minutes. We worked long hours in the bank, often without breaks, and it was past midnight before I got to bed and beyond one by the time sleep reached its dark fingers in to take me.

***

Six weeks later Fern was raped. She had been walking home from a film with some friends. The friends walked her to two blocks away from her street and told her they thought she would be okay making the rest of the trip alone. She wasn't okay. She was just one street over from her house, near a leafy green park that bordered the road when a man reached out of the shadows and grabbed her around the throat, placing his other hand over her mouth so nobody would hear her if she screamed or cried out. He dragged her roughly into the park, threw her down forcefully underneath a tree, yanked up her skirt, tore down her knickers and had his way with her. He left her discarded at the side of the park and told her if she told anybody what had happened he would lie in wait for her again some place when she wasn't expecting it.

"Next time", he said, "It won't be rape; it will be murder. Don't you dare open your trap to tell anybody about what's happened here tonight or it'll be curtains for you."

He drew one finger across his throat to demonstrate his point.

And then he was gone. Fern heard a car engine start, waited until she couldn't hear the engine anymore, then gingerly picked herself up and walked slowly home.

Once home, she acted. Smiled at her mother and sister, said she was tired and just wanted to sleep. She made her way to her bedroom and opened her laptop. I received her frightened message.

"It's me. Fern. I've been raped."

"WHAT??!!! When? How did that happen?"

"I was coming home from a film with some friends. We went our separate ways and as I was passing by a park near my house a stranger grabbed me and dragged me into the park. I feel violated. I need to take a long hot bath. I need a drink of something strong. But the worst part is he told me if I told anybody he would hunt me down and murder me. So now I have to live with that fear too. So you better not tell anybody else about it in case he comes after me."

"But Fern you need to go to the police."

"No way. If I do that he'll know I've narked and slit my throat. We have to keep this just between you and me."

It took me three days but I finally convinced her to go to the police. I knew it was the right thing to do.

The rapist had to be caught and punished or he would go on offending. The policeman who was put in charge of the case took extensive notes and offered Fern police protection which she accepted. She was asked if she wanted a man or woman to protect her and Fern asked for a woman. The woman, May, was to walk with Fern to work, to sit beside her at work and at lunchtime, to escort her home and to stay with her until she went to bed. At night, May would sleep downstairs in Fern's house. Fern told me she felt most reassured by this. Fern had described the rapist in as much detail as she could and the policeman in charge told her they would do their best to catch him.

Three weeks later she saw him. She was sitting outside her office with the officer assigned to protect her at lunchtime eating fresh spring rolls when she looked up and saw him staring at her. He held her gaze, then lifted his finger to his throat and drew it wordlessly, but threateningly, across. Then he turned and fled into the crowd. It was a hot day, but Fern shivered as though it was the middle of winter. She grabbed the policewoman's hand.

"I saw him", she said. "Just over there."

Fern pointed towards the crowd opposite.

"He stared at me and drew one finger across his throat. I told you he threatened to murder me, now he's stalking me at work. It's terrifying. He'll hunt me down and kill me."

Fern shook with fear.

The policewoman put one strong arm around her shoulders.

"It's okay honey. You're safe with me. He's just trying to psyche you out. I know it's hard but try not to let it get to you. Remember I'm with you 24/7 – there's not much he can do while I'm around. I carry pepper spray and a taser at all times. I'm well armed. Stick with me and I'll protect you. That's my job. My responsibility. It's what I'm paid to do."

Fern still felt shaken. She drew in closer physically to the policewomen, feeling the older woman's warmth through their shirts. I had given her my phone number when she told me of the rape and told her to call me if anything happened. She telephoned when I was also on my lunch break and informed me of the throat incident. I did my best to reassure her, though I too, was shaken by the event. How had he known where she worked? What else did he know about her? Did he know where she exercised and what restaurants she like to frequent? Did he keep a file? Did he have photographs of her at home on his computer? Just what kind of mind were we talking about here?

Back at work, at three-thirty-four pm I logged into my Facebook in order to try and provide Fern with some extra reassurance. I needed to let her know I was really on her side.

"I'll put my thinking cap on," I said. "I'll try and figure out his next move."

"Thanks", Fern wrote back. "I'm still feeling pretty frightened and finding it hard to concentrate on my work."

"Try and put that creep out of your mind", I said. "I know it's easier said than done but he doesn't deserve any of your mental energy. Just try and do a decent job this afternoon. Hold it together till 5.30pm. You don't want to lose your job."

Speaking of people losing jobs, my boss had seen me logging into my Facebook account and came marching over to my desk to give me my orders.

"That's it. You've had your warning. I don't tolerate disobedience in my employees. I need people who are loyal to the company, not people who waste time chatting up women during working hours. You're to pack up your desk and leave this afternoon."

He stormed off without another word.

So that was it for me. I was jobless. They wouldn't give me a reference and without one I knew I would find it hard to find work in Phuket or indeed, anywhere. Without work, how would I afford the rent on my apartment? I didn't want to go back to New Zealand, didn't want to admit defeat and go running back home to Mummy, tail firmly between legs. I wanted to prove myself a man. I had to make it in Phuket. I had to look the world in the eye.

Once home, I called up my best friend Mike who had come out from New Zealand at around the same time as me. Mike was a graphic designer who rented an office space in downtown Phuket. We met for a beer most Fridays and I knew I could count on him to help me out in a crisis. I asked him to meet me for a drink the next night. We met at Rockin' Angels with its walls decorated with album covers and I downed three vodkas before I had the courage to talk to Mike about everything that had been going on.

"I've lost my job Mike", I finally found the courage to stutter. "Which means I will be unable to afford the rent on my apartment. I don't have many savings, I've been living hand to mouth each month."

Mike put his arm around my shoulders and said the words I longed to hear, the words I had hoped and dreamed he would say. To be blunt, I had thought he might need a little more prompting.

"It's okay", he said. "You can stay in the spare room of my office. Just keep the place tidy and don't leave food scraps lying about or you'll attract rats."

"Okay."

I ordered another vodka to celebrate my newfound freedom and the fact that I still had somewhere to lay my head down at night.

***

Days at Mike's office were strange. I knew I should be applying myself whole-heartedly to finding another job, maybe even stooping so low as to fake references, or asking my brother back home to pretend I had worked for him in his roofing business, but my heart wasn't in it. Instead I found myself drifting aimlessly around Kata and Karon beaches, eyeing up women, with Fern in the back of my mind. I wondered what she looked like in a bikini. Although I wanted to, I still hadn't found the courage to ask her out on a proper date. What if she rejected me? Then how would I feel. Despondent and down and heel. Like one of life's losers, a reject, a retard. I bought a cheap camera and tried my hand at photography, taking snaps of the locals as they sunbathed or sipped drinks, or ate beef stir fry. I developed these photos myself, at night, purchasing the requisite chemicals and equipment and blocking out the windows in the small bathroom, to keep the light from the streetlights out. It was good to have a hobby – something to occupy my hands and time.

I contacted Fern to ask her how it had panned out with the creep. She messaged me back and said the police had caught him. He had been flashing an unsuspecting passerby and they had nabbed him, quite literally, with his trousers down. The case was still on trial but Fern had been promised by the police that he would be served a harsh sentence.

"The judges in this country don't look kindly on rapists. If I had my way they'd all get the death penalty, but not everybody takes my harsh view", stated the officer in charge of Fern's case.

Back at Mike's office, I began to grow lazy. Started sleeping in way past ten o'clock and not cleaning up after myself properly. I would leave half-eaten kebabs and old curries lying around despite Mike's warnings about rats. True to his word, the first rodent showed up sometime in July. I came home from an especially productive morning out with the camera to find it munching cheerfully on the previous night's kebab which lay discarded and forgotten in the corner. I was grossed out. I had been sinking slowly into the depths without really noticing what was happening to me. The rat forced me to face reality. I couldn't cohabit with a rodent! I had to get my act together. What if Mike found the rat! As if on cue, as if summoned by my thought, I heard footsteps upon the stairs. O God, I had to get rid of the rat before Mike saw it. I grabbed a smelly old T-shirt and made a dive for the furtive rodent but it screwed up its nose at me and scurried out of reach to the far corner of the room, which is where it was, still clasping part of the kebab, when Mike entered the room and saw it, clocking also the old, moulding food that so gracefully decorated the spare room of his office.

Mike was furious. I'd never seen him so angry. I didn't know what to say to placate him. What excuse could I make for myself? Unemployment had seen me turn into a slob par excellence and now I was ruining the spare room of his office he had so kindly lent me out of the goodness of his heart. What sort of friend was I? Give me an inch and I took a bloody mile.

"I'm sorry", I said. "I've been slipping slowly but surely into depression. Forgetting to shower. I think I need to see somebody. Maybe even a shrink, somebody heavy duty. I'll get rid of the food right now."

I began gathering up the old kebabs and curries and throwing them into the overflowing trash can in the far corner, right opposite the rat.

Mike lowered the tone of his voice.

"Listen, Stefan, I hate to break this to you, but I don't think you can stay here if you're going to live like this. When I offered you the flat I thought you were a tidy guy. Maybe it's my fault for not checking up on you often enough, for just leaving you to your own devices, but I trusted you. Aren't friendships supposed to be built on trust? I feel you've violated my trust Stefan, taken advantage of my generosity. Have you even done any cleaning at all? You're living like a complete animal, obsessed with that damned photography and forgetting to take care of yourself. I hope there's no hard feelings but I'm going to have to boot you out. Tonight. Pack your bags Stefan, you'll have to find somebody else to bludge off."

No hard feelings?! Mike's words hurt. He had called me a bludger and stated I had taken advantage of him. I hadn't intended to do so, it was just that lack of gainful employment had lowered my self-esteem and made me lazy and weak.

I threw the lid of the trash can at the rat then sulkily pack my bags. Where was I supposed to go? I was a loner and didn't have any other friends. Looked like it was the street for me, with the alcoholics and the derelicts and the other down-and-outers. I didn't look back at Mike as I exited the building.

***

Days on the street were tough, but the nights were tougher. I slept in a doorway two blocks over from Mike's office and he would sometimes pass me on his way to work. I had grown a full face beard by now and if he recognised me he didn't let it show. Probably he was ashamed of me. I was ashamed of myself.

You had to become hard to survive. Sad but true. My first week living rough, I was robbed. My last fifty dollars was taken from my wallet and I had no money to buy food. An unlucky squirrel crossed my path and I was quick enough to catch it with my bare hands. I slit its throat and skinned and gutted it with a hunting knife which had been a twenty-first birthday present from my father. I cooked it over a small makeshift fire which I built in front of my doorway. The next day I pawned my laptop and my camera, my only semi-valuable possessions. They were well worn and I didn't get much for them. My mobile still had a small amount of credit left on it so I telephoned my mother and begged for money and she put $1000 in my bank account. I didn't want to ask her for more. These were the years in which I was supposed to be proving myself, standing on my own two feet. Leaving the nest, I had not flown, I had fallen. Now I lay broken in the street.

I remembered Fern but was too embarrassed to contact her in case she asked about my living circumstances. I could lie, of course, but what if I got found out. That would be terrible. I wasn't a liar by nature. Lies just got stuck on my tongue. I wasn't clever enough for lies. Liars have to be able to think quickly or they get caught in a sticky web of their own deception. Since childhood I had figured that honesty was always the best policy and since I was deeply ashamed of the way I was living, I decided it best not to contact Fern.

I tried to be strong. Told myself that I would get through this. This was just a passing phase, just a nasty patch to endure. I went to internet cafes during the day and looked for work. I was desperate and would take anything. I bought a razor and shaved myself in the men's public toilet, then took to the streets in search of work. Anything would do. The hours spent without employment were too long. Time looped and dragged and wrapped itself around my useless fingers. I went into cafes, the zoo, the aquarium and various animal shows such as the snake show and Crocodile World.

Eventually the man running the snake show took pity on me and said I could work on the door taking money and clipping tickets. Never have I been so grateful. No more aimless wandering of the street. This would give focus to my life, give me somewhere to go during the day and provide much needed social contact. My life was sadly lacking in human relationships. I hadn't got to know many of Phuket's other homeless people – they tended to be loners, and each one kept largely to themselves. They did not operate in packs which was a pity as it may have given them a greater chance of survival.

One night I went to an internet cafe and contacted Fern. Much to my surprise she'd gotten married. I was taken aback and a little hurt. It wasn't that I'd imagined she'd marry me but I had felt we had some kind of understanding. Perhaps I had imagined it, maybe it had all been in my mind. Most nights I felt alone, felt a sort of empty pit in the centre of my chest but I did my best to cover it over by burying myself in work and I tried not to let my emotions affect me too deeply. That was the best way. Emotions were a waste of time. They only led to trouble. Wasted tears, bitter years.

The snake show was a sad affair. The tourists came in droves but many left disappointed. The snakes'd had their fangs broken and were drugged. The men running the show completely lacked empathy and compassion and gave no thought to the quality of life of the snakes who were being abused. The Phuket zoo had a similar reputation for animal abuse and I had not visited on principle. It was hard for me to work at the snake show, for although I was not complicit in the abuse of the snakes I knew what was going on and said nothing which in a way made me party to what was going on. My silence made me guilty. I took the money, clipped the tickets and went home at the end of the day feeling somehow unclean.

I worked at the snake show for six months and made enough money to rent a room sharing with two Thai men. The unit was small and grotty but it was a roof over my head and for that I was grateful, especially after having experienced life on the street. With time I forgot about Fern and I even found a girlfriend, an Australian called Sally, who I met one night at Rockin' Angels, drunk on Mojitos. Sally had curly sandy blonde hair and brilliant piercing green eyes like a cat. Life was looking up and my time on the street became just a dark nightmare I did my best to try and forget. Having met Sally, maybe I would even have to rethink what I had thought previously about emotions.

I was sitting in Neko Cat Cafe one day when I saw an advertisement in an open newspaper looking for donations to the Thai Society for the Prevention of Cruelty to Animals. I still had $700 in my bank account, left over from the $1000 my mother had sent me and I handed in my notice at the snake show and reported them to the Thai Society for the Prevention of Cruelty to Animals. I don't know if the society ever investigated or if anything came of their investigation if they *did* look into it, but it was a weight of *my* conscience and I felt at least I had done the right thing by the snakes.

***

My brother said he would lie and vouch that I had worked for him in his roofing business which meant I could apply for more meaningful work. He wrote me a glowing reference on company letterhead and I began to feel more secure. I had no experience but how hard could roofing be? I put some credit on my mobile and telephoned a few roofing firms and Lady Luck must have been smiling on me that week for I found a job at Chayond roofing working for Arthit, which means Man of the Sun. The name was appropriate for Arthit could be found up on Phuket's roofs in all weathers, and I was soon up there with him. Arthit had no fear of heights and would climb the steepest pitches to get the job done. I learnt on the job, learnt quickly and was soon working with asphalt, galvanized steel and shingles right alongside Arthit. The job made me as strong as before I had been weak, and I never wanted to face a period of unemployment again. Unemployment rotted the soul. Arthit also had excellent balance which made him perfect for the job. He was a natural born roofer and told me it was the job he had dreamed of since being a young boy.

"I used to climb up on our roof with my Dad when I was young to fix the chimney or the TV aerial. Used to love it. Loved the view. You could look out over all the other houses and feel like king of the world."

There was an art to aligning the shingles. You had to get them just right or the water, and wind would get through. We also installed insulation and vapor barriers and sealed everything off to avoid leaks. Arthit was a good teacher and I was happy to learn from him.

My girlfriend and I were getting on well. I was happy to have found a companion in life and was thankful I no longer had to walk such a very lonely path. Sally was good company and was an expert in making me laugh when I got stressed. As I grew to trust her I told her about my time on the street and her eyes filled with empathy.

"Oh, that must have been rough", she said. "At least those days are behind you now. You've got a good career in roofing if you play your cards right. It's a good steady job. People will always need new roofs and their old roofs mended."

I became a work robot and began to dream of running my own roofing business in Thailand. In the internet cafe I looked into the legality of it and saw I was entitled to start my own business there. This gave me some hope for the future. I felt I would be good at being my own boss. I wasn't really cut out for working for anybody else. Although I had turned into a slob when unemployed I could also be very disciplined when I wanted to get things done. Running a business would be good for me.

I took a night course in book-keeping, as I wanted to be able to keep the financial side of things straight and then I went into business as Stef's 4 Roofs. I was the little red hen. I did everything myself. I purchased all my own equipment and a white van which I had specially spray-painted with Stef's 4 Roofs in gold lettering on the side. I quickly picked up business, being careful not to poach Arthit's customers and soon had a solid customer base which kept my cash flow steady. At night I would crash into bed exhausted, setting my alarm for 6am the next morning when dawn would bring another hard working day.

Throughout my time as a roofer I had been getting closer and closer to Sally. We had been sleeping together almost every night for the last six months and in January of the following year I proposed. I was very nervous. I had bought an expensive engagement ring – an emerald surrounded by six diamonds from one of Phuket's most exclusive jeweller's and I was hoping she was going to say yes. I had kept the receipt for the ring and checked the returns policy just in case she turned me down. Nonetheless, I was quietly hopeful. She had told me she loved me on more than one occasion and I had reciprocated. We had a warm, close relationship – the kind of relationship I had thought I would never find in my life, which had been largely cold and empty, like a vacuum in outer space.

I took her out to the Blue Elephant, and after the mains, when dessert had been ordered but had not yet arrived, I did the old fashioned thing and got down on bended knee and proposed. She accepted with a coy smile and afterwards, when we were walking home, gave me a big smoochy kiss. My heart skipped in my chest and it struck me that I had found, in this harsh, unforgiving world, some small sliver of happiness and contentment.

Well, who can ask for any more than that?

The Orphanage

I took the job in the orphanage on a whim. I lived in Peckham and had been working in a café in East Dulwich. Walking home from work one evening I had seen the advertisement in the orphanage window.

Looking for fulfilling full-time work?
We are now hiring individuals
to help in our orphanage. You will
be assisting with the adoption process -
both bringing children into the
orphanage and adopting them out.
You will also be assisting with the
day to day running of the orphanage.
If interested phone 20 8693 2766.

I added the number to my contacts in my phone and headed home to my flat, then made a simple meal of chicken pasta and salad and dined alone.

The next day I phoned the orphanage. A gruff voice answered after three rings.
"Hello can I help you?"
I took a deep breath.
"I'm enquiring about the job", I said. "My name's David Thorburn. I've always wanted to work in an orphanage."
"Great. You can find us at 232 Lordship Lane. Bring ID and 2 references – one character reference and one work reference. Can you come in at around 4.30 today."
I said that this would be fine, as it would be after my café job had finished.

During my lunch break at the café I called the father of my friend Heidi and asked for a character reference. He said he would write me one and send it through via email. At 4.30 I headed to 232 Lordship Lane and knocked upon the door. The door swung open on its hinge and a slightly frumpy, frazzled looking woman appeared in the doorway. She held out her hand for me to shake.
"Hello", she said. "I'm Marian, Marian Hammond."
"Hi", I said. "I'm David. I rung this morning about the vacant position."
"Come in", she said, stepping to one side.

I entered, wiping my shoes on the mat, and followed her down the hallway which was wooden floorboards covered by a thin, threadbare carpet. Entering her office, the first thing I noticed was that the walls were adorned by photographs of babies and young children that I assumed were the adoptees.

Sitting at her desk, she paused and looked me up and down, then gestured towards a seat opposite. Obediently, I sat. Butterflies danced in my stomach. This was more daunting than applying for the café job had been.

"So what makes you think you'd be suited to working in an orphanage?" she asked.

"I'm really good with children. I have two nieces and I love them dearly. As a matter of fact, I was an orphan myself. I was adopted out when I was two. Could you please tell me a little bit about the role?"

"The role is varied. At times you will be helping us with the care of the children. At others you will be doing paperwork, helping out with the administration side of the adoption process."

"That sounds fine to me", I said, in what I hoped was a congenial manner. She then stared at me with a cold look, silence thickened in the room. The thought occurred to me that this woman hadn't smiled or laughed in a long time - years maybe decades.

She stared at me again.

"So, do you want the job or not?"

I hesitated not sure what to make of this lady.

"Sure," I said "Ill give it a go."

She handed me some forms.

"This is the job description and contract. Can you start on Monday?"

"Not a problem." I said "Thank you for your time."

I held out my hand for her to shake hoping to extract some warmth from this woman - She ignored my gesture.

At home I set about reading the paperwork she had given me, the job description first. Twenty or so pages stapled together at the top right hand corner. The content was very rigid and formal in style. Sentences such as 'Must be at work 15 minutes before your shift starts' and 'You must make sure the children are well behaved and quiet at all times' But the one that took me by surprise the most was '*No affection to be shown to the children at any time.*'

I supposed they had their reasons for their policies but it seemed a bit draconian. I signed the contract - the wage was seven pounds an hour - less than I was getting at the café however I'm sure this would be a more satisfying job. I felt sorry for the children (no affection – how brutal!) and hoped that maybe I could make a difference in their harsh lives.

Monday rolled around and I got up at 6am to be at work by 6:45am. Entering the orphanage it was chaos about five children were sitting in the hallway crying, two were fighting over a toy. I was met at the door by a child about two or three who looked at me with woeful eyes and immediately clung to my leg giving me the tightest leg hug imaginable. "Hello buddy." I said as I patted his head and prised out of his grip. I walked to the office to meet Marian she didn't even say hello just shoved a piece of paper in my hands proclaiming "This is the morning routine, it needs to be followed to the tee." Then she walked out.

Looking at the list the first thing on it was; *Breakfast in the dining hall all children must eat all that is given to them.*

I walked down the hall to find the kitchen, encouraging the children I walked past to follow me. They dutifully obeyed. Entering the dining hall I discovered three long tables with children sitting impatiently while two frazzled looking staff members were darting around serving breakfast - bowls from the kitchen which contained some sort of substance that looked like porridge.

I walked into the kitchen to see how I could help where I found what I assumed to be the cook madly spreading margarine on a row of toast. She glanced at me and then said "Can you get the jam out of the fridge please."

Helping her to spread the jam I then took platefuls of toast out to the tables where the children all grabbed greedily as if they hadn't eaten properly in months. Plastic cups of water were intermittently spilt across the tables, water gathering in puddles and dripping to the floor.

I sat down next to a baby who was crying and had an empty highchair tray. Picking up a piece of toast I put it in her chubby hands and she ceased crying as she started chewing on it with her only two remaining top teeth. With jam smeared on her face she grinned at me.

I wanted to shine some light into the existence of these children. Their lives were so dark and gloomy with no fun or laughter that it sent a shiver down my spine.

I read the next instruction on the piece of paper Marian had given me.

After breakfast all children must wash their faces and then be gathered together in the main dining room.

When it appeared that everybody had eaten something I ushered the children out and up the stairs to the bathroom. I pushed face flannels into their hands and tried to ensure that everybody had a good wash. After a flannel throwing fight broke out instigated by a boy with the most cheekiest grin I've ever seen, I managed to calm everyone down and usher them haphazardly to the main dining room as per instructions.

With all the children sitting around the tables noisily talking amongst themselves the atmosphere changed as soon as Marion entered the room. The poor tots looked frightened and immediately became silent.

"Well children," she exclaimed "It's Monday and you have had all weekend to clown around. Like the rest of the world you have to go to work, we have twenty two cars arriving today that will need cleaning inside and out and if I see any mucking around like last time you know what will happen."

A visible shudder ran through the children. I whispered to Lettie one of the other staff

"What *will* happen?"

"The dreaded time out room," she said in a hushed whisper "I'll show you later."

"Right get to it." Marion said as she exited the room.

Lettie and Sharon gathered up the children and we all filed out of the dining hall to a cold laundry. Stacked against the walls were about thirty plastic buckets – they were filled with cold water. Taking some of the buckets outside, I saw about twenty cars parked in the carpark. The children had dutifully followed us outside, some carrying buckets, some clutching scrubbing brushes. Lettie squirted a drop of dishwashing liquid into each bucket and with woeful expressions the children set to cleaning the cars.

I grabbed a spare scrubbing brush and set about helping.

Lettie came over and tapped me on the shoulder. "No, No, No." she said "Marion doesn't let us help the children with their jobs."

I couldn't watch, it seemed so wrong - a cold morning with cold water the children becoming saturated and shivering.

"So tell me about this time out room" I said to Lettie.

"C'mon I'll show you," she answered.

Following her inside we walked through the laundry, down the hallway, turned left and came to a door painted black with a wire mesh glass window. Opening the door, Lettie and I walked inside. The room was completely bare and as dark as night because the walls were also painted black.

On the opposite wall to the door was a small high window with bars letting in only a minimal amount of light.

"So what's the story with this?" I asked

"This is her punishment room," came the reply. "This is where the children get sent when they're naughty, they don't have to do much for Marion to put them in here, sometimes for hours at a time."

"But that's child abuse!" I exclaimed, shocked at what I was hearing.

"Nobody knows what goes on here, Marion keeps it all hush hush. She puts on a good front for the inspectors and trains the children what to say, threatening them with the time out room if they say the wrong thing, she's a nasty piece of work, she thinks she's got it all sewn up. If you want to keep your job I suggest you keep your trap shut about what goes on in this place. Marion doesn't take kindly to blabber mouths."

As I stood looking into the room shocked at what I had heard, a child's pleading reached my ears. Coming down the hall, turning the corner,

Marion approached dragging a child no older than three or four behind her.

We stepped aside as Marion shoved the child into the room slamming the door shut and locking it with one of the many keys attached to the lanyard around her neck.

Turning to us she spat "The dirty little brat soiled himself, you would think by that age they would be able to control their bowels, well he can sit in his dirty pants and think about it. Lettie come and get me in three hours, I think that will give him enough time to learn."

With that she turned on her heels and strode off. I stood outside the door in shock, I could hear the boy's wails from inside the cell like room. I felt Lettie's hand on my arm. "C'mon." she said gently. "There's nothing we can do Marion is the only one with the keys. It breaks my heart too."

The next three hours were long, Lettie took me to the staff office and showed me how to do some paperwork, while Sharon supervised the children outside cleaning the cars. I could barely concentrate. I kept an eye on my watch and as soon as three hours was up I informed Lettie and she went off to inform Marion.

I took the time to have a look around the rest of the orphanage, I discovered the nursery where the babies were occupied. They sat three or four to a playpen like chickens in a coop. They sat looking miserable half- heartedly playing with dirty looking broken toys, that looked like they had come from the dump.

I spoke to the first lot closest to me and they looked at me with hope in their eyes. One of them stretched out her arms for me to pick her up. I instinctively reached down to pick her up, ignoring the first policy I had read that children were not to be shown affection at any time.

At that point I didn't care, the child needed a hug and I was a firm believer in the power of love and affection in a cold cruel environment. The little girl smiled at me and snuggled into my chest like it was the first hug she had had in a long time, if ever.

It was then that the plan started to evolve in my mind that I would have to report this lady to social welfare because what was going on here was so wrong. I resolved to make the call later that evening from home. I spent the rest of the day formulating in my mind what exactly I was going to say to social welfare.

I went to help the cook prepare lunch. The children all filed in at twelve o'clock, wet, cold and looking exhausted. Lunch consisted of deep fried luncheon sausage, no fruit, or any of the nutrition children need. They got a miniscule portion each - however they scoffed it down like they were starving and appeared unsatisfied afterwards.

The little boy who had been locked in time out came in and sat down. He had tear mark stained cheeks. I went to the kitchen to get him his lunch. It was then the cook informed me that she had had strict instructions

110

from Marion that he wasn't allowed any lunch today. I saw red and decided to slip him some of my lunch. I sat down next to him and gave him some of my lettuce and marmite sandwich with the other kids looking on longingly.

Lettie, Sharon and I cleared up after lunch. We then took the children to their beds for their afternoon nap. As we were walking back down the stairs I asked Lettie "So do the children get any of the profits from the clients who got their cars washed?"

"Hell no." came her reply "Marion keeps that for herself." I was shocked.

At the end of the day I took myself off to Marion's office to sign out, She was sitting behind her desk which was covered in a pile of paperwork. Motioning with the pen in her hand towards the chair she indicated for me to sit down. I sat.

"So how did you find your first day?" she asked

I hesitated. What should I say, I hated it, it was the most disturbing day of my life.

"Fine." I lied.

"Well." She said turning to her computer, she turned the screen towards me.

"Do you realize I have security cameras in just about every room?"

Silence thickened in the room. It dawned on me then that I was in trouble. I remained silent. I wasn't going to explain myself to this horrible woman.

She tapped away at the computer keyboard and an image of the nursery came up with me picking up the crying baby earlier in the day.

"You broke the no affection rule. And later…" tap tap tap went her fingers. "Then you gave that boy some of your lunch."

I stared at her as she stared back at me. "Look." I said slowly "I really don't think this job is going to be for me."

"Yes, well that was to be expected." She answered. "You obviously don't have what it takes to work here, you're too soft. I'll put your wages for the day into your bank account however you will not be receiving the whole day's pay as you broke the policies."

I didn't bother to reply, I rose from my chair and walked out leaving the door open behind me I couldn't wait to get out of there.

Once home I made myself a cup of coffee, sitting at my laptop I wrote out the events of the day vowing to myself that I would take the information to social welfare the next day.

The following day I called up social welfare and made an appointment. I was given a slot with Kylie at 3pm that same day. I waited until 3pm then dressed in a tidy shirt and trousers and made my way to the social welfare office. Kylie was dressed in a smart black tailored suit, teamed with red lipstick. I clutched onto the notes I had brought with me. She sat down behind a desk shaped like a bean and gestured for me to sit down on the other side. Obediently, I sat. I handed her the notes and she read over them slowly her eyes slowly widening the more she read, her mouth hanging open.

"This all sounds very horrific", she said. "Thank you for bringing this to our attention. Rest assured that this matter will be thoroughly investigated. Thank you for coming in to see us."

"That's great", I said. "Thanks very much for your assistance."

On the way home I called in at the café at which I had previously worked and they gave me my old job back.

Three months later I saw the report on the six o'clock news.
Orphanage manager Marian Hammond was today brought to justice following more than a decade of abuse towards children. Interviews with staff combined with CCTV footage showed children being locked in seclusion rooms for up to twenty hours at a time, children being denied food, children being made to do slave labour without pay and children denied all affection. Marian refused to give a statement, appearing without remorse. She was stone-faced in court. She was sentenced to five years imprisonment. All children have now been placed into caring foster homes.

I was happy with this verdict and wondered whether Marian would learn her lesson in jail. Was she the kind of person who could be taught? How had she become so abusive herself? I found myself wondering about her own background.

A few weeks later the young boy who was locked in seclusion came into the cafe with his new foster family.

"Hey", he said, reaching out his hand to me. "It's the man who gave me a sandwich when I was hungry."

He gave me a big smile and said he was happy now and well cared for. I was pleased that at least one strand of the story had a happy ending.

Solitary

They locked me away. Said I was not fit to live among the humans. The judge said I was 'a danger to self and others' and that I had a 'seriously diminished capacity to take care of myself'. I was diagnosed and labelled, medicated and shoved into the corner. Forgotten about. Society's refuse. For six months I remained in that tiny cell like room. There was a small window carved into the wall. Meals, served on a paper plate, with plastic cutlery were pushed into the room by an anonymous figure in a white uniform at 7.30am, 12 noon and 6.30pm. I was treated worse than the lowliest dog. I had no company in my cell and, being claustrophobic, I sensed the four walls closing in around me. I feared I would be locked in there forever – a prisoner for all time. A prison sentence has an end date, but you can be kept in a psychiatric institution indefinitely – until such time as they deem you 'well' enough to be released.

I had committed no crime. I'd broken up with my boyfriend three months before being sectioned and had been smoking heavily and not eating properly, but surely there were many other women like that and you would not think that would give them a reason to lock me away from society's eyes. I had been paying my bills. I had not harmed anybody. I was pregnant to my boyfriend but he did not want to take any responsibility for the baby. He barely wanted to know me. On the way to a book club event, I had gotten lost in my car down some country back roads and knocked on a farmer's door for help, asking for directions. I must have looked disheveled because the farmer did not help me, they turned me away, lost, into the cold dark night and I was left to stumble around the countryside in my car. I never did find my way to the event. I was upset with my boyfriend, who had dumped me and I went around to his house one night to try and talk about the relationship. He told me he never wanted to see me again. I was in despair and the futility of the situation hit me. I went outside and lay down in the road and waited for a car to run over me. My boyfriend called the local mental health team to come and remove me. They came for me in their car, shoved me roughly into the back seat and put the kiddie locks on. I felt so demeaned!

I was driven to the local mental health unit where I was assessed by a cold clinical female psychiatrist who said I would have to stay in hospital for an initial five days and would not be allowed to leave. I felt that my rights had been taken away from me. This was compulsory detention! I was shown to my room, a small featureless room exactly like all the others on the ward. Thank goodness there was a window on the outside wall that looked out on a bland courtyard, which was edged only by a strip of grass, with no flowers or interesting flora at all. I blamed my boyfriend for sending me here. He had over-reacted when he had called the mental health crisis team. I had not posed any danger to him – I had never acted violently throughout our entire relationship.

I did not come from the best background. My mother had been an alcoholic and I was taken off her at the age of eleven and put into foster care. I can't remember if I was abused or not; most of the time is a blank. My Dad was a fisherman who had been in port for the weekend; my mother didn't even know his last name.

The five days were excruciating. There were phone calls from my distressed parents and sister who wanted to know what was going on. I told them that it was Matt's fault but that I hoped to be out soon. The psychiatrist banned me from making outgoing phone calls so that I could not contact a lawyer. It transpired that this was illegal, a fact that I found out upon my release, six months later. I asked my mother to arrange for a lawyer to call me, but the doctor must have blocked this call because it never came. I was in limbo, rotting. My frustration boiled up in me, nobody was listening to me. When a staff member approached me and told me I smelt and needed a shower, I snapped and picked up a chair and threw it at them. That was it. I was frog-marched into seclusion, the door was slammed and locked behind me. Because it was seclusion, it was an automatic no visitors zone.

The psychiatrist wrote in my notes that I must stay on the ward for a further 14 days, which seemed like a lifetime. She came to visit me in my locked cell and told me they were seeking an inpatient compulsory treatment order and that I would have to go to court. I had never been in trouble with the law in my short twenty-five years and I was scared. I had just had a cup of tea and I threw up on the spot.

Court date was set for two days time. I was so nervous - what was going to happen? The day came and two nurses came to usher me to court. Once there I had to wait in the waiting room for what seemed like an eternity. No-one talked to me I just received contemptuous looks from

114

whoever walked past me. I was under constant supervision by the two nurses as well as the burly looking security guard. I was feeling very discriminated against. I started to feel deep shame and anger welling up inside of me. A deep sense of injustice hit me. Why was I being treated like this? Like a criminal. My appointed lawyer had met me only briefly. I wasn't impressed with him. He looked about eighty and carried a frayed old briefcase with a whole lot of crumpled papers hanging out of it and he reeked of whiskey and stale tobacco.

"I've been assigned your case, I only got time last night to have a quick look over the notes and I have to say it's not looking very hopeful." Then he walked off to the reception desk and I overheard him ask where the free coffee was.

Eventually it was my turn to enter the courtroom. The judge didn't even look at me as I walked in with the nurses. He was busy reading his notes with his glasses perched on the end of his nose. I sat down and all was silent. My lawyer stumbled in with spilt coffee down his shirt and notes from his briefcase falling on the floor. My psychiatrist was present, already seated.

The judge spoke.

"So are you Miss Cathy Haroldson?" he said, still not looking at me. I remained silent. How arrogant, I thought. I decided not to answer until he looked at me. Silence thickened the air. He didn't look at me for two minutes but continued rifling through his papers.

He looked up "No answer? OK I'm holding you in contempt of court, which means you are more likely to get an inpatient order. Would you like to tell me your name now?"

Something snapped inside of me.

"You have my name in the notes you arrogant bastard." I replied.

He slammed his hand down upon the desk.

"I will *not* be spoken to in that manner. Young lady you are sentenced to a six month inpatient order and I am advising the doctors that you spend it in seclusion."

I gave him a cold look. I was not going to give him the satisfaction of bursting into tears although I felt very despondent.

I was lead back to my cell by the two nurses who had brought me out.

"That's not going to help your case, talking to people like that", said one of the nurses.

"I don't care", I snapped back.

It was true. I was beyond caring. I just wanted to lie down and be left alone.

Left alone I was – for days, weeks, months on end. Like a caged animal. My parents and sister were not allowed to visit me and there were no phone calls allowed. For approximately 183 days I was cooped up in there – the silence broken only by the sound of a meal being passed through the flap or somebody coming to give me medication. I passed the time by singing to my baby, wondering what side effects the psychiatric medication would have on my child. I was also scared that they might take my baby from me once it was born.

The psychiatrist in charge of my care came to visit me once a week. My medication was increased to keep me more doped up. I expressed my concerns about my baby's welfare but they still forced me to take the medication in front of them.

The first note appeared after I had been in seclusion for a month. It was slid under the door one morning shortly after breakfast and was written on lavender scented paper. It read 'Hold on. You are very brave. Thinking of you. B.'

I was taken aback. Somebody was thinking of me? The note was a light shining into my darkness. It was the only kindness anybody had shown me in a long time.

My six months passed with only the notes to hold onto.

'Thinking of you and your baby. I know what you must be suffering,' read one.

'Hold on for a brighter day', read another.

I came to look forward to them, and treasured them and hid them under my pillow. Who was writing them? Some kind soul. And brave too, to risk being found passing notes in such a clinical, intimidating atmosphere.

When they finally let me out I was very subdued, my head hanging down low, feeling very uncertain. As I was standing in the reception area, ready to transition to the world outside, a nurse came up to me, put her hand over mine and pushed lavender paper into my hand with messages written upon it - 'I'm here for you if you need me' and an address. 'Please be discreet' was written at the bottom of the note. B. I was taken aback by the human contact. Our eyes met. Contact was made. I was intrigued – she had held out her hand to me. I wanted to know more.

I'd had a casual job as a receptionist at the local backpackers and was owed a month's wages. I also needed somewhere to stay. They were forthcoming with the money. I booked myself into a single room, then called Work and Income to make an appointment. I mused to myself that it went against human nature to be locked away in a small room. In the morning I stood opening and closing the door for five minutes, marveling that I had this small power – the power to let myself in and out of a room. I was now seven months pregnant and was unsure as to what my next move would be. The world outside seemed scary and dangerous, devoid of friends, and it was not just me now I had to think about my child as well. I took out the piece of paper that the nurse had handed to me. I smelt the paper, the lavender scent reassuring me. I went to the local service station and found a map, to locate the address. I then caught a bus to her house.

The house was a three bedroom bungalow with a beautiful garden filled with lavender and roses out the front. A black cat with green eyes greeted me at the gate. I bent down to stroke it and it meowed in a friendly manner. I approached the door, hesitating before ringing the doorbell. Gathering my courage, I pressed the buzzer. The door swung open and there stood Bridget. She looked different out of her uniform. I guessed that she was about forty. She had light wrinkles around her lovely green eyes. Her red hair fell to her shoulders in a wavy bob.

"Hello there, I was wondering if you'd come and see me."

She stood back so that I could enter. I entered the house.

Inside the house was warm and inviting with polished wooden floorboards and walls painted cream with an apricot frieze. Bridget fixed us both a cup of coffee, then told me I could stay in her spare room for as long as I wanted.

"Just till you find your feet love. I wouldn't want to take your independence away, but sometimes it's nice to be cared for. Especially after you've been through an ordeal."

After we had finished our coffee she showed me to the spare room. It was painted up like the other rooms, which I found comforting.

The Italian film festival came to town and Bridget and I attended many films together. We would go out to dinner together afterwards. I had been locked in solitary for so long that it felt strange to be leading a 'normal' life – dinner and a movie and it took me some time to adjust to being in 'the world outside'. I often felt that people were staring at me, even when they weren't. I also suffered many nightmares about being buried alive and would cry out in my sleep. Bridget would then come into my room and rub my back and prepare me a cup of hot milk to soothe me.

I felt overwhelmed by Bridget's generosity and did not know how I could repay her. I had nothing to give. I did my best to help out around the house and not to get underfoot. We started going to the beach together too, taking picnics with us. In short, we derived enjoyment from life. My pregnancy was progressing and I was by now in my eighth month with an enormous bulge sticking out the front of me. Bridget took me shopping for baby's clothes, a bottle, a pushchair, a basinet and a cot. She said it was good to be prepared.

One night as we sat up late talking Bridget confided in me that she had always wanted to have a child but could not conceive. She was infertile. Her husband had left her because of this problem.

"Not much of a husband", I scoffed.

"He wanted children too and I couldn't give them to him, so he moved on."

"What about adoption?"

"My husband was fussy. He didn't want to adopt. I wouldn't have minded it."

I asked Bridget if I could have a homebirth and she agreed that I could.

The night of my childbirth rolled around. The midwife was called and arrived with oxygen and painkillers. I grunted and groaned on the bed in the spare room, and eventually the baby was born. She was gorgeous and I named her Sophie. Bridget said Sophie was a welcome addition to the household and swore to care for her as if she was her own – the child she had always wanted. I was glad to be able to make Bridget happy – to give her a child. So Sophie grew up with two mothers. I stayed living with Bridget for the next ten years. When Sophie went to kindergarten I went back to work at the backpackers and could pay my way, so with time I felt less reliant on Bridget and more capable of standing on my own two feet.

I tried to put my days in solitary behind me and build a new life, a life of light and laughter, but in dreams I would remember it, and even ten years later, Bridget would still come in to soothe me at night with a cup of hot milk, and rub my back and attempt to make me tranquil and tell me that everything was going to be alright.

Hitch

My mother always told me not to pick up hitchhikers. She said they were dangerous. She said you never knew who you could be taking into your car. She always said I was too trusting, too naive and that other people would take advantage of me, exploit me throughout my life. Perhaps she was right.

Hello my name is Cindy and I was jilted by my boyfriend while heavily pregnant. The trauma caused a miscarriage at 6 months. Blood everywhere. 'Never forget it.' I had thought that the two of us would be an item for life; I was not expecting to be dumped. There was no doubt that the baby was his – I am not a tart, I do not sleep around. I don't know why he ditched me; he didn't give a reason. Maybe I got on his nerves or he thought I was too much of a bimbo. I don't have a glamorous job, I'm just a secretary at P&S Legal, a dull job by anybody's standards, a job that 85% of the population could do with their eyes closed.

After being dumped I went through a stage of reading numerous self help books, searching for answers to the riddle of life. Then I decided that it was all about treats. Life could only be borne if you had regular treats. One of my treats was taking routine trips to Hamner Springs to soak in the hot pools and rest my tired bones. Getting out of Christchurch after the earthquakes was good. The earthquakes had taken a toll on the regional psyche – there were nervous breakdowns, more crime and dissatisfied hyper-sensitive youth galore.

It was on one of these trips that I decided to pick up the hitchhiker. He looked down and out, and was standing on the side of the road with his thumb extended. It was just opposite The Pines beach. I pulled over, leaned across, wound down the window and asked him where he was headed. He replied that he was travelling up North to Nelson. I said I could take him as far as the turnoff to Hamner. The date was November the 9th; we had just celebrated Guy Fawkes. After he had been in the car for about ten minutes, he withdrew a lighter and a sky rocket from his back pack and began to fiddle around with them, flicking the lighter on and off near the fuse of the rocket. This made me uneasy to say the least and I told him so. He put the sky rocket down on the floor in front of him, but took out a Swiss army knife from his bag and flicked it open. I nervously cleared my throat.

"Excuse me, would you mind putting that away while I'm driving?"

"Look love", he said threateningly. "I need to get to Nelson tonight. I had a shitty sleep last night in the pines and I'm feeling real grumpy. I'm not one to be messed with."

I didn't like the way he was talking to me. It reminded me of the way my ex-boyfriend used to speak after he'd had a few drinks. I drove a little further and pulled down a side road under the pretence of needing to go to the toilet. Luckily for me it was a secluded area with trees providing shade and shelter; the perfect setting. I told him to get out of the car and fortunately for me he obeyed. I didn't want to make a mess of my vehicle. I karate chopped my victim in the throat, then, while he was still numb with shock wrestled his penknife off him and stabbed him in the jugular. Blood spurted everywhere. I dragged the body from the car and left it under the trees. I picked up his backpack, looking for money and was pleased to find ten thousand dollars in cash. Our boy was cash rich! A haul for me. I drove away feeling satisfaction at a job well done.

The money I took later to an orphanage – it's what I always do with the cash.

They came looking for me. Some nosey parker had noted down my license plate number when they saw me parked 'suspiciously' amongst the trees. I got away with it. Said I murdered in self-defence. Said that he attacked me. The cops bought the line.

Later that week, when I was back at home I saw the report on the six o'clock news.

"Escaped convict Daniel O'Brady has been found dead en route to Hamner Springs. Mr O'Brady was known for theft of over 30 vehicles in the Christchurch region and had escaped from Christchurch men's prison last Wednesday. The killer has been found but not prosecuted as police say she murdered in self-defence."

Thankfully there was no picture of me on the news. That would have interrupted my modus operandi. With every hit I was honing my skills.